THE *Christmas* RING

Also by Karen Kingsbury

Someone Like You

Just Once

Forgiving Paris

In This Moment

Love Story

Two Weeks

Truly, Madly, Deeply

When We Were Young

To the Moon and Back

A Distant Shore

Between Sundays

Divine

Fifteen Minutes

Like Dandelion Dust

Oceans Apart

On Every Side

Shades of Blue

The Baxters—A Prequel

Redemption

Remember

Return

Rejoice

Reunion

(and many others)

For a complete list of Karen Kingsbury titles, visit KarenKingsbury.com

KAREN KINGSBURY

THE *Christmas* RING

THOMAS NELSON
Since 1798

The Christmas Ring

Copyright © 2025 by Karen Kingsbury

All rights reserved. No portion of this book may be reproduced, stored in a retrieval system, or transmitted in any form or by any means—electronic, mechanical, photocopy, recording, scanning, or other—except for brief quotations in critical reviews or articles, without the prior written permission of the publisher.

Published in Nashville, Tennessee, by Thomas Nelson. Thomas Nelson is a registered trademark of HarperCollins Christian Publishing, Inc.

Thomas Nelson titles may be purchased in bulk for educational, business, fundraising, or sales promotional use. For information, please email SpecialMarkets@ThomasNelson.com.

Scripture quotations are taken from The Holy Bible, New International Version®, NIV®. Copyright © 1973, 1978, 1984, 2011 by Biblica, Inc.® Used by permission of Zondervan. All rights reserved worldwide. www.Zondervan.com. The "NIV" and "New International Version" are trademarks registered in the United States Patent and Trademark Office by Biblica, Inc.®

Publisher's Note: This novel is a work of fiction. Names, characters, places, and incidents are either products of the author's imagination or used fictitiously. All characters are fictional, and any similarity to people living or dead is purely coincidental.

Any internet addresses (websites, blogs, etc.) in this book are offered as a resource. They are not intended in any way to be or imply an endorsement by Thomas Nelson, nor does Thomas Nelson vouch for the content of these sites for the life of this book.

ISBN 978-1-4003-5476-4 (HC)
ISBN 978-1-4003-5477-1 (epub)
ISBN 978-1-4003-5478-8 (audio download)

Printed in the United States of America

25 26 27 28 29 LBC 7 6 5 4 3

Donald, my Prince Charming, the man of my dreams. Thirty-seven years married to you is only the beginning, my love. Thank you for always cheering me on, always loving me, and always believing in God's miracles. I couldn't be me without you. I love you with all I am.

To my children and grandchildren, who prove to me daily—over and over again—that God's greatest gift really is love. I cherish the laughter in our moments together and your kindness and intentionality in every possible way. I'm proud of you beyond words, of your faith and passion and creativity. I love you and I love this life we share. I never imagined this would be my story. But God has blessed us and made it possible. What a life!

To my mom, who has been there through every stage of my writing journey, and who still loves my reader friends and the people getting adoption grants from our One Chance Foundation. I cherish the time, Mom. I love you.

To my sisters, who have also worked alongside me from the start. Isn't this the most fun any family ever had? I love you and I thank God for you.

And to God Almighty, who has—for now—blessed me with these.

Chapter 1

June 6, 1944, 12:45 a.m.

IN THE DARK OF night and against the sound of enemy fire, the moment he jumped, rushing wind hit Bill Bailey square in the face. He pulled his parachute cord but even as it opened, he could already tell. Something was wrong. The C-47 transport plane ahead of them—the one labeled "Stick 66"—was turning around trying to get back to base.

Bill winced. Anyone could see the plane wasn't going to make it. Long before his feet hit the ground, he watched through the clouds and fog as the plane plummeted into a French hillside. The explosion took Bill's breath. His platoon had known the details wouldn't play out perfectly like they'd rehearsed. But this?

One name after another raced through his mind. Guys he had laughed with and tossed a ball with and shared letters from home with. Some of them from his hometown of Columbus, Georgia. Fort Benning.

The loss happening right before him was more than Bill could comprehend. All that training in England had led to this. And now nearly twenty of Easy Company's best and bravest were gone.

Don't think about them, Bill told himself. *Don't look.*

He set his face forward, the flames behind him. Bill's parachute sailed through the dark sky over Normandy. *Focus. Don't get distracted.* In the dim light the sky was peppered with other paratroopers, others from the elite army group. "Screaming Eagles," they called themselves. Bill tried to steer his parachute to an open field.

That's when it happened. Gunfire ripped through the air all around him, bullets grazing his arms and legs and the top of his helmet. So close he figured he must've been hit. His heart pounded and for a single moment all he could see were the faces of his mother and father. His two sisters. He could smell the roast his mom had made the night before he left.

"You'd better come home!" his oldest sister had told him. "Don't fall in love with a French girl."

He was never going to see them again, and he was only eighteen.

The barrage of bullets continued and it still felt like a million miles till touchdown. Another problem became clear. Bill was drifting. He wasn't so much making his way to the ground as he was flying sideways. Sideways far from the coastline and straight through enemy fire.

Time slowed and he wasn't parachuting into France in the middle of the night ahead of the Normandy invasion. It was yesterday again. He and the other Screaming Eagles were pouring out of a war movie and the lieutenant was directing them to tables with documents.

"Sign them," he had shouted. "All of you. Sign them."

Bill found a spot at one of the tables and saw what they were about to sign. Life insurance policies.

"Half of you won't make it home." The lieutenant's voice had grown stern. "But never mind that. The mission ahead is the one you were born for. Do not worry about tomorrow."

Do not worry about tomorrow. The same words Jesus had told His disciples. Words written often in the Bible. *Do not be anxious. Don't be afraid. Do not worry. Be strong and courageous.*

The ground was finally rising up to meet him. *Do not be afraid,* he told himself. *God will see you through.*

But as the heels of his boots dug deep into the ground, Bill knew two things. First, he was nowhere near Utah Beach. And second, God had not seen many of them through after all. Because next to him two of his closest buddies lay in a heap beneath their ripped-up parachutes, dead before they'd hit the ground.

Nausea hit Bill like a kick to the gut. He reached out to help his friends. As if he could bring them back. But as he did, another spray of bullets flew over his head.

He had to get out of here.

He struggled to break free from the nylon and ropes.

Gunfire and German voices cried out all around. From deep inside his backpack, Bill found his knife. He hacked at the parachute cords until he was free. Then he shoved the nylon into a bush and ran. Ran as fast and as hard as he could until the next round of gunfire ripped across the night.

The bullets were not aimed at him this time. But the sound was deafening all the same.

Bill scrambled into a bush—and found five of the Screaming Eagles.

"Shh." One of them grabbed his shoulder. His voice was little more than a whisper. "Don't speak."

Bill shook his head. Not a word.

His eyes adjusted a little more. He knew these guys. He'd shared a bunk room with three of them. More gunfire and then Bill realized what else he was hearing.

The sound of men being hit. Men dying.

Finnie sat across from him. Finnie Eastman. Bill looked at him and shrugged. With barely a sound he uttered, "Where are we?"

"Some village." Finnie opened his backpack and pulled out a canteen. The others did the same. Water could mean the difference between life and death.

Not until the canteens were put away did Bill realize that every one of his guys was injured. The worst was Woodsy to his right. Bill grabbed a roll of bandage from his bag and cut off a long piece. He wrapped it over the gaping bullet hole in Woodsy's leg. Then he nodded. Woodsy would be fine. He had to be fine.

Bill settled against the base of the bush and closed his eyes. How had this happened? Easy Company had flown in low from the west, a part of the 2nd Battalion of the 506th Parachute Infantry Regiment of the 101st Airborne Division. Georgia boys. American through and through. The army's bravest. Easy Company's Screaming Eagles.

Strapped with eighty-pound packs, Bill figured they would drop almost rocklike to the ground. No time to be shot at. Instead, with the wind and weather, they had bounced around like barely weighted balloons.

The goal had been to land near the target: the Cotentin Peninsula just off Utah Beach. Commandeer it from the Nazis and prepare the way for the land invasion coming at daybreak. Instead, they were trapped in a bush somewhere in the French countryside with a battle raging all around them.

Bill still didn't know how they'd survived this long.

With morning still forever away, Bill did what the others were doing. He closed his eyes again and tried to find the peace he needed to survive the night. What was that speech the captain had read before they boarded the planes before dusk yesterday? Words from General Dwight D. Eisenhower. Bits and pieces darted through Bill's mind.

"You are about to embark on the Great Crusade, toward which we have striven these many months. The eyes of the world are upon you . . . Your task will not be an easy one. Your enemy is well trained . . . He will fight savagely . . . The tide has turned! The free men of this world are marching together to Victory! . . . Let us beseech the blessing of Almighty God upon this great and noble undertaking . . ."

Explosions popped off not far from them, and then the sound of more men being wounded, more men lost to the battle. Bill blinked. Lights from the falling bombs were visible through the branches of the bush where they were hiding. Reds and silvers and golds.

Like Christmastime.

Would he be home for Christmas this year? Would he make it out of this bush? *Home.* Ever since he'd landed in

England, it had become his favorite word. Bill let it fill his head and heart. *Home.* He held on to the feeling and images it brought to him.

Christmas hadn't been the same since Pearl Harbor, but it was still his favorite time of the year. As long as he was home.

Gunfire rang out, closer this time. Bill shifted. *I'll never be home again.* Not for Christmas. Not ever.

His backpack slid out from beneath him and he started to go with it. Without making a sound, Bill dug his fingers into the soft dirt and tried to straighten his bag. Tried to get it to cooperate. And that's when it happened.

The tips of his fingers on his right hand brushed against something buried in the ground, something cool and solid and metal. Bill turned and made more of an effort. When his gear was again straight against the base of the bush, he found the spot in the dirt. Whatever was there, it had been buried long ago. Another try and he pulled the item free and stared at it. Still encased in mud its shape was hard to make out, but it felt familiar. Like a ring.

He brushed it against his army pants, pushing away the encrusted soil and polishing the metal over and over. Finally in the dim light of the distant bombs he could see it. A deep gold band and a ruby-red stone. The jewel was ringed with a circle of glimmering diamonds.

Bill stared at it. Where had the piece come from and how had it wound up buried here beneath an overgrown shrub? He checked his buddies. They were half asleep, bleeding, and scared. One of them took another sip from his canteen. Bill stared at them. Who would still be alive in the morning?

He leaned against his backpack again and clutched the

bauble tight in his hand. Somehow the ring gave him hope. Like God hadn't forgotten him and the other guys from Easy Company. The red ruby was a sign.

Images filled his head, flashes of his future, maybe. He could see himself being rescued from France and helping the Allied forces win the war. And in time he would meet the sweetest girl and they would fall in love and get married. Then he'd take her home. Home to his parents and his sisters and their first Christmas together.

They would have a family and—

An explosion rocked the earth beneath him. Bill sheltered Woodsy. His leg wasn't bleeding out anymore, but it wouldn't be long. Would any of them live to see the morning? To be rescued?

Sleep finally won out. Bill had no idea how much time had passed, only that when he opened his eyes, the sun was shining and distant gunfire filled the air like a hailstorm back in Columbus. A few of the guys were awake, shivering, holding on to each other.

The land invasion had begun.

But where were they hiding, and what had happened to the peninsula? Bill peered through the bushes and there on the bluff was an old church. If they could make it across the field, they might find shelter until US troops came for them.

"Hey!" The voice was American. Hands tore the branches away and a face stared at the six of them. "Let's get out of here. We need to get you boys to the medic."

Bill noticed the flag on the man's uniform. It was the most beautiful sight he'd ever seen.

"Woodsy, wake up." Bill helped the group grab their gear and crawl out of the bush. "Finnie, come on."

The soldier led them to a truck and suddenly they were headed away from the war and straight to an Allied fortress where they could be treated and cared for.

They had survived. They were free.

Not till they were climbing out of the truck did Bill realize he was still holding the treasure he'd found in the dirt. He studied it for a long moment. This single object was proof God had been with him all along. He must've seen what Bill was going through and known what Bill was feeling. How badly he was missing home.

The piece of jewelry was proof.

Yes, one day he would marry that girl, whoever she might be, and they would raise a family and this ruby-red gem would always serve to remind him that God had spared Bill Bailey on D-Day for a reason. He would keep the ring in his family for generations to come. He could see it all playing out before him.

Bill smiled. He even knew what he would call it.

The Christmas ring.

Chapter 2

THE FOUR-DAY CHRISTMAS TRIP to Breckenridge, Colorado, turned out to be exactly what Vanessa Mayfield and her daughter, Sadie, needed. They were staying at The Village in a condo with views Alan would have loved. There was something sad about that, almost as if it would've been easier if the place had no view at all.

But sadness aside, Vanessa was enjoying this trip with Sadie. The two of them had decided it was okay to take this vacation even though Alan had only been gone four months and they were both still grieving. Besides, they would carry Alan with them always. Wherever they went. Forever.

Sunshine streamed through Vanessa's bedroom window that winter morning. Vanessa breathed deep, stepped out of bed, and stretched her legs. Two days of skiing had taken their toll, but she didn't mind. Sore muscles meant she and Sadie had enjoyed every minute on the slopes. Skiing was something the Mayfield family had done every December since Sadie was a little girl. As long as Alan wasn't deployed.

This was their first time here without him.

Vanessa had asked God to give him a front-row seat from heaven.

She walked to the window and pulled open the sheers. The sight took her breath. If paradise had a quaint small town in the snowy mountains, it would have to be Breckenridge. The town lay spread out before her, the historic district and antique shops, and beyond that, the perfect ski runs.

Rays of sunlight hit the diamonds on her hands and cast sparkly lights across the windowsill. Vanessa glanced down. She still wore her wedding ring, probably always would. And, of course, the Christmas ring.

Vanessa lifted her hand and studied the antique.

The understated red-ruby center and the circle of pretty diamonds around it. All of that set in a dark gold band. No telling how old the relic was. Vanessa only knew that her great-grandfather had found it on D-Day after he and a handful of other paratroopers from the 101st Airborne Division landed in a French field outside of the village of Sainte-Mère-Église.

Somehow, he had found the ring buried in the ground beneath a bush, where he and his buddies hid until they were rescued that day, eight miles north of Utah Beach.

Vanessa ran her finger over the smooth red stone. The stones weren't real. Vanessa's mother had taken it to the local Columbus jeweler decades ago to make sure. "Beautiful," the man had said. "Costume jewelry was more exquisite back in the mid-1900s. Especially in Europe."

Everyone had suspected as much, not that it mattered. The value of the ring would never come from an appraisal.

The ring had been in the family since D-Day, passed on from her great-grandfather to her great-grandmother. And then to her grandmother and after that to her mother, who had given it to Vanessa on her college graduation.

Sadie was fourteen now. In four short years she'd be off to college, and four years after that, the Christmas ring would be hers.

"Mom, I made eggs!" Sadie's singsong voice came from the kitchen.

Vanessa slipped into jeans and a turtleneck and followed the sound.

Sadie was a mirror image of her father: fair with his blonde hair and blue eyes. Nothing like Vanessa, except for her smile. As soon as Sadie smiled, everyone said she and Vanessa were practically twins.

Over breakfast, Sadie was quiet.

"Thanks for the eggs." Vanessa recognized her daughter's sad expression.

"You're welcome." Sadie smiled, but her eyes welled up.

Until now their days together on this trip had been marked with silliness and full-on laughter. Like the time Vanessa slid backward—skis in the air—down the end of the run their first day here.

This moment was very different. Vanessa reached for Sadie's hand. "You okay?"

"Don't you wonder"—Sadie put her fork down and lifted her eyes to Vanessa—"if God could've protected Daddy, how come He didn't?" She hesitated. "He could've kept him safe, right?"

Give her time, Vanessa told herself. *Don't rush this.* She ran her fingers over Sadie's hand. "Yes. I do think so. I think He could've kept Daddy alive."

Sadie's shrug made her look like a little girl. "Then . . . why?"

This was the hardest part about being a military family. Or the family of a police officer or firefighter. By merely doing their jobs, they put their lives on the line every day. Any goodbyes could be their last. Vanessa studied her daughter. Not every question needed an answer.

"I know the right things to say." Sadie paused. "There are no guarantees when your dad's in the army . . . and he's not the first medic to get killed helping someone. God was with him. We'll see him again." The hint of a smile lifted Sadie's cheeks. "I actually believe all that."

"We're taught to look backward." Vanessa kept her tone soft, thoughtful. "To be thankful for the time we *did* have him . . . and not angry about the time we *won't*." Vanessa sighed. "It's hard for me, too, honey. It'll always be hard."

Sadie picked up her fork and moved it around her eggs again. "I know he's with Jesus. And we'll all be together again someday."

"We will." Vanessa waited until she could feel Sadie's mood lift a bit. "I keep thinking . . . if Daddy has a window up in heaven, I sure hope he missed my fall the other day."

A ripple of laughter seemed to catch Sadie off guard. She took a bite of eggs and pointed her fork at Vanessa. "Mom, it was so funny! Your skis shot straight up in the air."

And like so often on this journey of grief, the two of them were okay again. Laughing and recalling Vanessa's spill in detail.

"Listen, Sadie girl." Vanessa finished her plate and cleared it to the kitchen. She was still laughing. "Don't think I'm taking the big sledding hill today. Not happening."

"Oh, come on! You can do it!" Sadie brought her plate to the kitchen, too. "At least one time!"

The laughter remained as they left The Village and headed out. Carter Park was known for its many sledding runs and free stash of sleds at the base of the hill. Breckenridge was a family-friendly town, and by the time Vanessa and Sadie parked and reached the bottom, the place was crowded.

"Let's go, Mom." Sadie grabbed a sled for two people and led the way to the tallest hill. "I'll help you."

Vanessa had no doubt she could make the climb. She ran two miles a day and followed the same morning workout she and Alan had done together since they got married. "The question isn't whether I can get *up* the hill." Vanessa trudged behind her daughter. "But whether I can get down."

"Without flipping, you mean." Sadie laughed again. She picked up her pace.

Vanessa kept up. "If I do flip, please don't ever make me sled down this mountain again."

The two of them arrived at the top, and Sadie turned to her. "Mom." The wind was harder at the crest. "You're my best friend. I want you to know that."

For the rest of her life Vanessa knew she would remember this moment, out of breath standing by Sadie about to slide down the longest hill at Carter Park in Breckenridge. Her daughter's sweet fourteen-year-old smile and the gift of her words just now.

"You're my best friend, too, Sadie girl." Vanessa gave Sadie a side hug and felt the cold brush against her hands and arms. Only then did she realize she'd forgotten her gloves in the car. "No!" She held up her hands. "I'm going to freeze."

This only made Sadie laugh harder. ""Mom. It's Colorado. How could you forget your gloves?" She couldn't stop laughing. "You're the funniest person I know."

"That's my goal." Vanessa shook her head. "What am I going to do with myself?"

"Just hold on to me. My jacket will keep your hands warm."

So that's what they did. Vanessa sat in the back with Sadie in front of her. The drop looked far too steep, so Vanessa closed her eyes and hung on to Sadie. Her daughter was right. Sadie's jacket kept Vanessa's fingers as warm as if she'd had her gloves.

The ride to the bottom of the long hill seemed to take forever. Vanessa screamed the whole way down, and Sadie giggled. That's when it happened.

They were almost to the bottom of the hill when out of nowhere a little boy ran right in front of them.

"Stop!" Vanessa screamed, but there was nothing they could do. They had to hit the child or ditch the sled.

"Roll!" Sadie threw herself sideways and Vanessa did the same thing. They fell off the sled face-down in the snow and flipped another five times before stopping. From the corner of Vanessa's vision, she saw the little boy run off, unaware.

Vanessa looked at Sadie, her face inch-thick in snow, hair matted with ice. "Where's your hat?"

Sadie felt for it and again she started laughing. "Mom... you look like an actual snowman."

Together they scrambled for Sadie's hat and slid on their backsides the rest of the way down. At the base of the hill, they were laughing so hard they could barely make it off the course. When Vanessa had cleared the snow from her eyes and nose and had caught her breath, she bent over her knees. "That might be the most fun I've had at Carter Park."

Which was why they went back to the car for Vanessa's gloves and then did the sledding run again and again and a fourth time before stopping for lunch. Over burgers and fries Vanessa listened as Sadie shared drama from her freshman class. "The seniors are so mean. They think they rule the school."

Vanessa raised her brow. "Well..."

"Okay, true." Sadie grinned. "But still..."

They talked for almost an hour, and the whole time Vanessa studied her daughter, letting her laughter etch itself deep within her heart. In a place where it would live forever. Because the teenage years did not last forever. They had an expiration date like everything in life.

Even being in love with an army medic.

If the Lord allowed, she and Sadie would come back to Breckenridge again next December and the next and the December after that. But one day Sadie would fall in love and get married, and these sweet and silly mother-daughter trips would come to an end. Not that they would never take a trip together after Sadie married. But it wouldn't last this long. And it certainly would not have the laughter of this trip.

After lunch they took another few runs down a more modest hill, and then they built a snowman on the field near the parking lot. "Look. He's an army Ranger." Sadie eyed the snowman. He had leaves for ears and sticks for eyes and a mouth. Sadie turned to Vanessa. "Don't you think?"

Vanessa folded her arms and nodded, sizing up the snowman. "Definitely an army Ranger."

The sun was making its way toward the mountain ridge, so they headed back to the car. They ordered pizza for dinner and watched *Scrooge*, the musical. When the movie ended, Sadie wiped tears from her cheeks. "I think about the people you and Daddy have helped, on the battlefield and at church. Older people especially. Some of them found life because of you two." She smiled. "I always picture a few of them being like Scrooge. Given another chance at life."

Vanessa pulled her daughter close. "I can see that, too."

"But Daddy already knows." Sadie sniffed. "Because a lot of those guys you two helped are in heaven with him."

"So wise." Vanessa studied her. "I had the best time with you, Sadie girl."

"I had the best day with you, too, Mama."

Again they hugged. They would leave in two days to make it back to Columbus, Georgia, for Vanessa's first annual Columbus Cares Military Dance on the 23rd. But in the time that remained, it was difficult to imagine any day topping this one.

Vanessa replayed the fun of the afternoon as she brushed her teeth and washed her face. Not until she went to put lotion on her hands did she realize the most horrible thing.

Her Christmas ring was missing.

Sadie could tell something was wrong, and instantly she joined Vanessa in searching the floor and then her bedroom and then the sofa where they had watched the movie. But the whole time Vanessa knew she wouldn't find it. Not in the condo. The ring had always been a little loose when her hands were cold. Her heart sank. She must have lost it tumbling in the snow. Probably the first time she went down the highest sled run.

For a moment she thought about finding a flashlight and driving there now. Spending the night looking for it. But the park was closed.

Instead, in the morning she and Sadie got permission to search the sled run before it opened to the public. "We have to find it, Mom—we have to." Sadie crawled on her hands and knees next to Vanessa.

"We will. I believe we will."

"Pray." Sadie kept moving, kept searching. "God knows where it is."

Practically frantic, Vanessa prayed. "Lord, please lead us to the ring. It's been in the family for generations, and it has to be here somewhere. You know where, dear God, so please . . . lead us to it."

They prayed and they prayed and they prayed for most of an hour until finally the park operator had to open the runs to the public. "You find it?" he called out to Vanessa and Sadie.

"No." Vanessa gave her number to the man. "Please. Could you call me if someone turns it in?"

The man agreed and they trudged through the snow to the car. Once inside, Sadie hugged Vanessa and they both cried. Sadie looked devastated. "I'm so sorry, Mom. It'll turn up. I know it will."

"Maybe if I offer a reward." Vanessa's heart was broken. Losing the family Christmas ring was almost more than she could take. How could this even be happening? The whole experience was a nightmare from which she would certainly awaken.

But every time she checked her hand, the truth remained.

She and Sadie found a photo with the ring on Vanessa's finger. They zoomed in on it and took a screenshot and made a flyer. Then they spent the afternoon passing out copies to every antique shop, pawn store, and thrift building in Breckenridge. They posted flyers at The Village office as well.

The woman at the counter was kind. "These things have a way of turning up." She smiled at Vanessa. "I believe you'll find it. One way or another."

"Oh, I believe. I do." But she knew as well as anyone that believing didn't mean things would go her way. Otherwise Alan would be here helping them look.

In the car on the way back to Denver International Airport the next day, Vanessa and Sadie held hands. They were quieter than before. The only thing Vanessa could think was that with every mile they moved farther from her missing heirloom. Finally, as they drove home from the

Atlanta airport, an overwhelming thought hit Vanessa and there was nothing she could do about it.

The Christmas ring was gone. She didn't need a search effort to find the family antique.

She needed a miracle.

Chapter 3

Four Years Later

FROM THE TIME THE doctor placed infant Sadie Anne in Vanessa's arms, she and Alan had known their hearts would never be the same. Two years later, when it was clear Vanessa couldn't have more children, she and Alan agreed that one thing would for sure mark the years of raising Sadie.

They would make every day count, each hour a treasure. Because childhood never lasted long enough. She and Alan had understood this truth back then, and Vanessa certainly knew it now. Especially today.

Because this was the day Vanessa had dreaded and dreamed about for her daughter. The day she would move Sadie to Reinhardt University, the quiet, picturesque school forty minutes north of Atlanta. Sadie loved the countryside that surrounded the place, and though less than half of the Reinhardt applicants got accepted, Sadie had sailed through the process.

She'd been giddy about the fact since she received her

official letter. Not only that, but Sadie had been given a full-ride scholarship from the university's Military Gold Star Families program.

Vanessa grabbed one of the last boxes from Sadie's bedroom and carried it to the car. Sadie was a few steps in front of her. She glanced over her shoulder. "I talked to Bella. She'll be there half an hour after us."

"Perfect." Vanessa had hoped she might have time alone with Sadie.

This trip to college was early because Sadie had signed up for a two-week honors program. Vanessa was proud of her, but the decision meant less time together this summer. At least they had this morning, the two of them moving Sadie into her dorm. And now it seemed Vanessa would get the chance to meet Bella—the roommate Sadie had connected with shortly after being admitted.

Everything was all figured out except one thing: how Vanessa was ever going to get along without her.

Three more boxes and the car was packed. Vanessa sized up the load. "I think that's it."

"If it even fits in my dorm." Sadie laughed.

The new bedding and mattress topper, her dorm-sized trash can and laundry basket, and the posters she'd bought for her wall. A wildflower hanging with her favorite Scripture, a photo of their family back before Alan had died, and another one of Sadie and Hudson Rogers, her army Ranger boyfriend and the brother of her best friend, Ella.

All the items Sadie would need to feel at home. Everything except Vanessa.

A memory came to life in Vanessa's heart. The time she and Sadie went to Breckenridge the first Christmas after Alan passed. She could hear her daughter saying the words she'd said so often: "Mom, you're my best friend."

It was still true; Vanessa knew that much. Even if Sadie didn't say it as often as she once had. Vanessa gave the load a final push and closed the back hatch.

Sadie looked at Vanessa's hand. Then she took gentle hold of it and studied her empty right ring finger. "It'll be gone four years this Christmas." She lifted her eyes to Vanessa's. "No calls?"

"Not for a long time." A sigh came from the still-broken pieces of Vanessa's heart. "It's probably ten feet deep in the snow at Carter Park by now."

"I remember what you said that day." Sadie squeezed her hand. "God knows where it is. Do you pray about it? After all this time?"

"Every night." Vanessa could feel the fading sorrow in her smile. She would never give up on the ring, not as long as she lived. "Right before I go to bed, I look at my finger where it used to be. And I think about my great-grandfather and how important that ring was to him. And I ask God to bring it home. Some way. Somehow."

Sadie leaned in and kissed Vanessa's cheek. "That's all you can do!"

They grabbed cups of to-go coffee for the road and set out.

Reinhardt University was two and a half hours from Columbus, Georgia. That was one gift Vanessa was thankful for. Sadie would be close. Close enough for Vanessa to get in the car and take her to lunch or check in on her if Sadie got homesick.

Her roommate, Bella, was driving to school today, too. Bella lived south of Columbus, so she had already offered to bring Sadie home at Christmastime. Vanessa was counting down the days till then.

The drive to Waleska, Georgia, flew by. The crazy traffic of Atlanta gave way to quiet rolling hills and green pastures, and almost out of nowhere the campus appeared. By the time they had unloaded Sadie's things, her roommate arrived. Bella was quieter than Sadie, but the two seemed to hit it off.

"My parents wanted to come," Bella explained. "But they work for American Airlines and they're in San Francisco this week."

Since Bella needed help, Vanessa and Sadie pitched in to get her unpacked, and then the three of them worked to set up both beds. The dorm room was bigger than most, and each girl had her own desk. On hers, Sadie set up her family picture and the framed photo of her and Hudson.

When the beds were made and the room was ready, Bella seemed to notice the photo. Her eyes lit up. "Is that your boyfriend?"

"Yes." Sadie touched the edge of the frame. "That's Hudson."

"He's super cute." Bella looked at the picture again. "My boyfriend is somewhere on campus." She giggled. "At least I hope so." Bella sat on the edge of her bed. "How did you and Hudson meet?"

"It's a funny story." Sadie sat on the edge of her bed, too, so she was facing her new friend. Vanessa took the spot beside her daughter.

Sadie held the framed photo of her and Hudson and looked at it. "I've known Hudson since I was a little girl. His sister and I became best friends in third grade. Hudson was in sixth. I never thought of him as more than my friend's big brother until last Christmas. He had time at home after becoming a Ranger, and we hung out practically every day."

Vanessa smiled listening to Sadie talk about Hudson. The chemistry between the two was something that had grown over time, an attraction Vanessa and Hudson's mother, Peggy, had seen years ago. Hudson was older than Sadie, and very careful with her young heart. He was deployed now, but they talked often. Details Sadie still shared with her.

Of course, Sadie knew the risk of Hudson's job. She knew it better than anyone, and she loved him more because of it. That made the two an almost perfect pair.

Vanessa had a feeling Sadie and Hudson would stay together and that sometime after her college graduation the two would marry. Not that they were talking about that. Not yet. But again, Vanessa had a feeling. She could see it in the way Hudson looked at Sadie.

It was the same way Alan had looked at her.

Just after two o'clock it was time for Vanessa to leave. The girls had a welcome party at the gathering room, and parents weren't invited. Which made sense. Vanessa bid goodbye to Bella first. "I hope to meet your parents next time."

"My mom said the same thing. And she told me to thank you for helping me get things in order."

Sadie walked Vanessa out to her car, and for a moment Vanessa saw her daughter's entire life run through her heart in slow motion. Her infant days and baby stages, the time she learned to walk and go to school and say her prayers. The day she was baptized and her first week of middle school. Shopping trips and sing-alongs and dance parties in the kitchen.

And the terrible news of losing Alan. The trying to figure out how to live again that followed and the way his death had only made Vanessa and Sadie closer.

Vanessa could see it all. For what felt like forever, Sadie had been a part of Vanessa's every day, her very life, her constant thought. Until now.

From the time Sadie was born, Vanessa had prayed for her daughter to fly. And now it was time for God to answer those prayers. Time to let her go.

"Don't cry, Mom." Sadie slipped her arms around Vanessa's waist and laid her head on her shoulder. "I'll see you at Christmastime."

The hot Georgia sun pounded the pavement around them as the two held on to each other. Vanessa tried, but there was no stopping her tears. Finally, she put her hands on either side of Sadie's face. "I love you, Sadie girl. I'm a phone call away."

Tears filled Sadie's eyes, too. She nodded, and her sob became a laugh. "Maybe I'll just go with you. Forget the whole thing."

Everything in Vanessa wanted to agree with the idea,

grab Sadie's things, and take her back home. Instead, she kissed Sadie's forehead. "You're going to love it, honey. You will."

"I'll call you tonight." Sadie's eyes held hers. "Thanks, Mom. You're still my best friend."

"And you're mine."

With that, Vanessa hugged Sadie once more, climbed into her SUV, and drove off. The last thing she saw before turning onto the main road was Sadie. Still standing there, hand raised, waving goodbye.

Keep her safe, Lord. Vanessa turned her eyes to the road ahead of her. *Please protect her. Let her excel and grow and learn.* She blinked back fresh tears. *And help us both make our way to whatever is next.*

Not till she was on the highway halfway to Atlanta did she realize she was nearly out of gas. Vanessa dried her eyes and pulled off at the next exit. The one that read *Marietta, Georgia.* She had been to the charming town a few times before—always with Sadie. The city was great for mother-daughter trips and boutique shopping.

Down the street from the gas station Vanessa saw a store she hadn't seen before.

Millers' Antiques.

The shop had a welcoming front porch and windows that looked like they belonged in a house from a hundred years ago. Then she saw the sign: *Christmas-in-July Sale.* Vanessa pondered the idea. *Christmas in July.* She smiled and wiped her cheeks again. *Sure. Why not?*

This was her new life. Vanessa mustered her joy. She might as well make a memory out of the afternoon. Besides, maybe she would find her Christmas ring. Wouldn't that be something? She looked at her empty right hand. Back in the beginning, Vanessa stopped at every antique store and thrift shop she came across. Not so much lately. But why not?

What a Christmas-in-July miracle that would be.

She smiled. With God all things were possible, right?

Chapter 4

THEIR CHRISTMAS-IN-JULY SALE WAS something Ben Miller and his dad, Howard, did every year. Their nod to the memory of Ben's mom, who had been gone five Christmases this coming December. Word spread after the first few years, and now people came from all over Georgia to take part in the event.

The draw wasn't just that the vintage store items were on sale. Millers' collected Christmas antiques all year in anticipation of this event, so customers had come to expect they would find not only the best objects from the past, but also the best pieces from Christmases gone by.

As Charles Dickens would say, heirlooms from Christmas long past.

Ben watched his dad at the register. Their part-time clerk was Gary Owens, Ben's second cousin, his dad's first cousin. Both men were in their early seventies. Mainly, Gary showed up to play an ongoing mean game of chess with Ben's father. But days like this everyone at the store worked hard. The place was packed.

"Ben, I got something for you." His dad wore a Santa

hat and shorts. Sure, it was nearly a hundred degrees outside and the humidity was suffocating. But inside Millers' Antiques the air-conditioning was full blast, and it was indeed Christmas in July.

Ben jogged to the register. "I'm here. You need help?" The line was three people deep.

"We're good." He grinned at Ben. "Give me a minute."

A few feet away, Gary rang a bell. "Hundredth sale of the day!"

"Every time a bell rings . . ." Ben's dad winked at his cousin.

Gary didn't miss a beat. "An angel gets its wings." The two old guys were gray and goofy and good with antiques. Every day was a gift for them and for everyone who walked through the doors.

Ben loved working with them.

"Hot dog!" His father welcomed the next customer à la George Bailey. Then he turned to Ben. "Got a new box of antiques behind the counter. You wanna get 'em out on the floor for me please, son?"

"You got it." Ben found the box. Mixed Christmas dishes from an estate sale in New York. The pieces were finely etched with deep red and gold, a design that was likely from London.

This was what set Millers' Antiques apart. His dad knew how to comb the online estate sales and store closures across the country, so that every few days a box or two would arrive. Old treasures that would be picked up by their customers as quickly as he and his father could put them on the shelves.

Ben had seen himself going into finance when he graduated college two decades ago. The store had been his parents' idea, but when business began to boom, Ben's choice was an easy one. Why help a stranger's business thrive when he could help this one?

Gary came along even before Ben's mom had passed. The business had been a family affair ever since—and a lucrative one.

Weaving his way past the hundred-year-old Bibles and two-hundred-year-old typewriters, Ben took the box of dishes to the housewares section. He picked up the first plate and turned it around. Sure confirmed his guess. London, England, 1911. These plates wouldn't last a day.

With practiced care Ben set the dishes on the shelf, propping the prettiest of the group up on the display easels. He was still doing that when he heard a voice that caught his attention. He looked back at the register and tried not to stare. A woman had entered the store. She wore shorts and a T-shirt, and her long dark hair framed her pretty face.

Ben had an antique plate in his hand, and suddenly he had to remind himself not to drop it. She was talking to his father, asking something Ben couldn't quite make out. Whatever it was, the woman smiled and nodded. Then she headed straight for the Christmas jewelry section. Their store had one of the best displays of antique holiday baubles in the country.

His father walked with the woman and motioned to a counter of boxes. "Take your time. If it's here, you'll find it." He patted his stomach like Santa Claus. "Interesting things happen during Christmas in July."

The woman laughed. Her voice sounded almost lyrical. "Thank you."

More than half the customers who came into the store were female, and typically Ben did nothing more than direct them to the right part of the store. But something about this customer took his breath. Like he'd seen her somewhere before and had never been able to forget her.

Ben set the box of plates down and walked to her. She was sorting through a box of rings. He studied her for a moment and decided to have a little fun. "You getting married?"

She looked up, clearly taken aback. "Excuse me?"

He took a step closer. Was it just him or was her tone a little flirty? "You're looking at wedding rings. That's what you do when you're thinking about getting married."

"No." A slight blush colored her cheeks. "I'm not getting married. I'm . . . looking for something I lost. A ring."

As if they were the only two people in the store, Ben came up beside her and checked out the rings in the box. "What does it look like?"

"Antique gold. Sparkly with a red stone at the center. Small diamonds surround it."

"Hmm." Ben turned just enough to face her. "Beautiful."

The woman didn't catch his double meaning. She kept looking through the box. "It's not worth much. Except to me."

"Well . . ." Ben couldn't take his eyes off her. "I'm Ben Miller."

"Miller." The woman looked to the store register and

then back to Ben. "As in Millers' Antiques? Best Christmas heirlooms in the state?"

"Yes." Ben chuckled. "My dad and I own the place."

"Wow." She looked around, studying the displays. "I'm impressed." Her eyes found the register. "Was that your dad with—"

"The Santa hat and shorts? Yes."

This time they both laughed. Again, Ben felt it. Like he'd met her somewhere before. That's when he noticed the wedding ring on her left hand. He took the slightest step back.

The woman looked straight at him. "I'm Vanessa Mayfield."

"Hi, Vanessa." Now that he'd seen her ring, he wasn't about to flirt with her. "You live in Marietta?"

"Two hours south. Near Fort Benning. Dropped my daughter, Sadie, off at Reinhardt University an hour ago. Her honors program starts early." She shrugged. "I needed something to cheer me up. So here I am."

Ben allowed the moment to linger. "I'm glad." He had to ask, had to find out if she was taken. "So . . . you're already married?"

"No." A sadness flashed in her eyes. "Widowed. My husband was an army medic. He died in combat four years ago."

He hadn't expected that. "I'm sorry."

"It's not your fault." Clearly Vanessa had given this explanation many times before. She smiled at him. "What about you?"

"Also widowed." They were the same. This tragic exchange forever a part of who they were. "We were in our early thirties when it happened."

Her eyes held his. "Not many people get it."

Maybe that was why she had felt familiar. The fact that their stories were so alike.

"It's Sadie and me now, the two of us. I'm not ready to let her go." Vanessa sifted through another box of rings. "She always tells me I'm her best friend."

Just then Ben's dad came dancing down the aisle, carrying a tray full of plastic cups. "Gingerbread iced tea!" He swooped the tray toward Ben and Vanessa. "Help yourself!"

More laughter between them, and they each took a cup. Howard winked first at Ben, then at Vanessa. "People come back for the gingerbread iced tea!" He poked his elbow at Ben. "Isn't that right, son?"

"You got it, Dad. It's all about the gingerbread iced tea." He watched his father dance his way to the next customer.

"He's amazing." Vanessa shook her head.

"He is." Ben clicked his plastic cup with hers. "Cheers."

"Cheers." Vanessa looked through the rest of the box. "So . . . why the focus on Christmas? How did that happen?"

"My mom. But honestly it just made sense. Antiques and Christmas." Ben took his time. He didn't want this lovely stranger to ever leave. "Both bring yesterday to life again."

"Nice." She grinned. "You're a poet."

"Yeah. Sorry." He hung his head before meeting her eyes again. "Blame it on Walt Whitman. I'm a big fan."

"'Keep your face always toward the sunshine.'" She delivered the line like she'd said it a thousand times. "'And the shadows will fall behind you.'"

"Okay. Now I'm impressed." Ben wanted to check his feet to make sure he was still standing on the floor. But he maintained eye contact.

"Antique lovers and Walt Whitman sort of go hand in hand." She picked up a bracelet from a third box.

"Like poetry, antiques are proof that the past happened. That it was real."

"And it mattered." Vanessa's smile warmed his heart. "Even Walt Whitman couldn't have said it like that."

Their conversation continued. He asked about Sadie and the missing Christmas ring, how she had lost it and where she thought it might be.

"I pray I'll find it someday." She didn't look discouraged. "I'll always pray to find it." She told him how she still stopped into the occasional antique shop to see if it might be there. "That's why I'm here."

A wave of customers entered the store.

"Ben!" His father sounded panicked. "A little help, please!"

"Coming!" Ben looked at Vanessa. "Tell you what." He took out his phone and handed it to her. "Give me your number and I'll text you. Next time you're in town we can go antiquing. Look for your ring."

Her eyes sparkled. "I'd like that." She typed in her contact information and handed the phone back to him.

"I'll text you." He grinned and jogged off to the front of

the store. The best feeling came over him as he reached the register.

His dad was explaining to a customer the type of antiques the store bought. "These are not ordinary old goods." His father was passionate about the contents of their shop. "We sell treasures, ma'am. Within the walls of this place, you just might find a diamond in the rough!"

Ben thought about Vanessa Mayfield and his father's comment. He smiled to himself.

Indeed.

THE FIRST text from Ben Miller came before Vanessa reached her car.

Nice meeting you, Vanessa. Sorry you didn't find your ring . . . Maybe next time. Speaking of which, will you be back in Marietta? I can't promise gingerbread iced tea, but I'd love to look around with you.

She glanced over her shoulder at the storefront. Ben was helping an older gentleman near the front window. He looked out and for a moment their eyes met. Ben smiled and Vanessa did the same. Ben turned his attention back to the customer.

When Vanessa slid behind the wheel again, she realized her heart was pounding. She checked the rearview mirror. Her cheeks were red, her eyes bright with the thrill of the meeting. And a feeling she hadn't had since she met Alan more than two decades ago.

Infatuation.

"Calm," she told herself. She gripped the wheel and drove off. But the whole time all she could think about was the handsome stranger. The man had come into her life suddenly. Even if just for today. He looked familiar, and then she put it together. *Guardians of the Galaxy.* Of course. Last night she and Sadie had watched the movie—one of Sadie's favorites.

Ben Miller looked just like the lead actor from a popular TV series. Vanessa couldn't remember his name. The same dashing good looks and boyish charm. His athletic build and the easy way he had with conversation. Even the same green eyes, although Ben's might have been even more striking.

Vanessa Mayfield. Get hold of yourself. She sat a little straighter. She was acting like a schoolgirl with a first-time crush. Ben was a nice guy who lived more than two hours north of her. He had his own life and she had hers. They'd probably never see each other again.

Meeting him was nothing more than a diversion, a wonderful way to begin this next chapter of life. Life without Sadie living under the same roof.

But no matter how she tried to convince herself, she couldn't stop thinking about him. And she couldn't slow her racing heart.

At the first stoplight before getting back on the interstate, Vanessa texted Ben. *It'll be tough without the gingerbread tea, but I really would like to do more antiquing in Marietta. I'll let you know when I'll be back. Oh, and nice meeting you, too, Ben. Glad my missing ring brought me through the doors of your Christmas-in-July sale.*

The second she sent the text, she regretted it. Why had she been so forward? *Glad my missing ring brought me through the doors of your Christmas-in-July sale?* Who said that? The answer was immediate. Walt Whitman, that's who. Vanessa smiled.

Whatever the feeling rushing through her veins and heart, she liked it.

Before she could set her phone down, it rang and at first Vanessa thought it might be Ben. Then Sadie's name appeared. Vanessa steadied herself and answered the call. "Honey! How was the welcome party?"

"So good! Mom, the girls here are super kind. Everyone is friendly and we already made plans to find our own corner in the library so we can study together."

Peace filled Vanessa. Sadie was going to be okay. "I knew it. It's just what you and I prayed for."

"Exactly! I just got off a FaceTime call with Hudson, and he said the same thing. He knew it was where I was supposed to be."

Vanessa liked that. And maybe *she* was supposed to visit Millers' Antiques today. The thought took her breath.

"Mom?"

"Yes. Sorry . . . I agree completely. You're supposed to be there, and honey, you're going to love it!"

"Thank you." Sadie sounded concerned. "Are you still driving?"

"I am." Somehow Vanessa felt caught, like she'd done something wrong. "I stopped at an antique store in Marietta."

"Oh . . ." The tension in her voice eased. "Looking for your ring?"

"Exactly." Vanessa focused on the road. "They were having a Christmas-in-July sale."

"Got it." She hesitated. "Nothing?"

"Nope."

"Well, at least it was a fun stop."

"Yes. Yes, it was." Vanessa couldn't keep from smiling. "I saw a few nice things. It's a great store." She was careful to guard her words. Something she never normally did around Sadie. "I didn't buy anything. Just looked."

"We'll have to go when I'm on a break." Sadie sounded distracted now. The conversation about the antique store was behind them. Vanessa breathed deep, thankful. She wasn't even sure what had happened.

There was no way she could explain the situation to Sadie.

They talked a while longer about Sadie's classes and how she and the girls were going to walk the campus to see where they needed to be Monday morning when school started.

After the call ended Vanessa thought about exactly how fun the stop had been, how meeting Ben Miller had become the highlight of her day. When she parked her car in front of her house later that day, she felt her heart jump.

On the screen of her phone was another text from Ben. Before reading it, Vanessa lifted her eyes to the blue summer sky overhead. College wouldn't change anything between her and Sadie. They would still talk about everything. And in time, if she ever saw Ben Miller again, she would of course tell her daughter. Because the truth was, Vanessa had, in fact, found something at Millers' Antiques.

She'd found a new friend.

Chapter 5

INSTEAD OF FEELING LOST and alone with Sadie gone, Vanessa's friendship with Ben had become a life-giving source of joy. A gift she had never expected.

And now after five months of talking and texting and the occasional FaceTime call, along with two trips to Marietta for lunch and antiquing, Vanessa was hours away from meeting up with Ben Miller here.

In her hometown of Columbus.

But first Vanessa needed to wrap up the volunteer brunch at her house. The breakfast happened every year a week before the Columbus Cares Annual Christmas Military Dance. Like always, the dance was slated for two days before Christmas. It was a formal affair that included the community coming together to sponsor local military families who needed a little assistance at Christmastime.

Columbus Cares was Vanessa's heart project. It was a full-time job and involved a spring auction to support families and year-round availability for military families—meals for families when a soldier was welcomed home, and meals when a soldier was lost. Vanessa had developed a strong connection with local government offices, which allowed Columbus Cares to help connect widows and widowers with the benefits due them.

At a grief group for Gold Star Widows, Vanessa had met Maria Lopez and Leigh Collins—two Columbus women who had also lost their husbands in fighting overseas. The two of them had grown children in the area, but they also were financially able to spend much of their time volunteering with Columbus Cares.

The three of them came up with the annual dance. But it was Vanessa who took the organization personally. She remembered a long-ago conversation she'd had with Alan. "Military families should never want for anything," he had told her. At the time he had only been in the army a few years. He shook his head, clearly troubled. "Some of our people can barely put food on the table. I'd like to do something about that."

But Alan ran out of time.

Vanessa wasn't about to let his death be in vain, not when he had dreamed to do something so big. Alan wasn't only a medic and a hero, he was smart. He had left her and Sadie a significant life insurance policy. Between that and the money Vanessa received from her grandmother's estate and the army, she was set for life.

Financially, anyway.

Which meant Vanessa had all the time in the world to turn Alan's dream into a reality.

Columbus was one of the biggest military cities in the nation, and the need to help families of those serving had never been greater. This would be the fourth annual military dance. Like so often since Alan had left them, Vanessa hoped he had a front-row seat to every good thing Columbus Cares was doing in his memory.

Especially the dance.

This year their goal was to see a hundred families sponsored at a hundred dollars each. Not only that, but merchants across Columbus were donating goods and gift cards for baskets that would go along with the cash given to each family.

The task was quite an undertaking.

Twenty-some military wives had gathered this morning at Vanessa's house. Now the women were leaving, taking with them a list of what they still needed to do. The dance was in just one week, and the last several days would be spent decorating the Veterans' Hall. Vanessa and Leigh and Maria stood at the door and bid each volunteer goodbye.

When Vanessa finally closed the door, she glanced at the time. She was meeting Ben in one hour.

"Whew." Leigh dropped into the oversize chair near Vanessa's Christmas tree. "I think we just might pull it off."

Maria studied Vanessa's tree. "Twice as many families." She glanced over her shoulder at Vanessa. "Ambitious for sure."

"It is." Vanessa sat on the nearby sofa. "But we can do it. The town is behind us!"

"I need a snack." Leigh pulled herself from the chair and walked to the kitchen. "Where do you keep the cashews?"

"Top drawer by the pantry." Vanessa laughed under her

breath. Leigh was the cutup of the group. Maria, the more sensitive. And Vanessa, the one determined to make things happen.

Maria sat down near Vanessa. "Sadie comes home tonight?"

"She does. I can't wait." It was a lot for one day, but Vanessa had the timing figured out.

"Hey," Leigh called out from the kitchen. She held up a flyer for Vanessa's missing Christmas ring. "I haven't seen one of these in a while. You still handing them out?"

Vanessa and Maria joined Leigh in the kitchen. The three of them looked at the flyer. "I stopped a while ago."

Leigh studied the photo of the ring. "It sure was pretty."

"*Is* pretty." Maria gave Leigh a disappointed look. "We agreed to not give up on finding the ring."

Leigh made a doubtful face. "It's been a while."

"Still." Maria looked at Vanessa. "Whenever I think about it, I pray you'll find it, Vanessa. I do."

"I don't." Leigh raised her brow. "Can't lie to you, Vanessa. The ring's gone. Totally gone."

"Wow, Leigh. Not very kind." Maria shook her head. The two were like a sitcom when they were together. "You don't have to tell her you're *not* praying about it. Just keep that detail to yourself."

"Yeah, well. We have a lot more to pray about with the dance a week away." Leigh looked at the flyer again. "What's it worth, anyway? I never asked you."

"Leigh!" Maria's mouth hung open. "You don't ask someone a question like that."

"It's a perfectly normal question." Leigh turned to Vanessa. "Is it worth something?"

"No." Vanessa laughed. "Only to me. It's just a pretty piece of costume jewelry."

Maria raised her brow. "That's been in your family since World War II."

"Exactly." Vanessa stared at the ring. It had been so long since she'd seen it, since the piece had been on her finger. She took the flyer from Leigh and slipped it back into the drawer. "The volunteers are set." She sighed. "Let's figure out what we need to do to pull off this dance."

The three sat at the table and discussed decorating and band rehearsal. Again, Vanessa looked at her watch, then at her friends. "So . . . I'm meeting Ben today. Right after we're done."

"Ben? Ben who?" Leigh's face lit up. She was still chewing a handful of cashews. "Do we know this guy?"

Maria shot Leigh a look. "Ben Miller. Vanessa told us about him last week. The antique dealer from Marietta."

Leigh's eyes grew bigger. "Yes, yes, yes!" She swallowed her cashews. "The one who looks like that actor. How could I forget?" She took another two nuts. "When can we meet him?"

"Well." Vanessa smiled. "Tomorrow, actually. He's staying for a week." She hadn't told anyone this next detail. "He's taking me to the dance."

"What?" Leigh was on her feet. "Like a date?"

"Sit down." Maria tugged on the sleeve of Leigh's sweater. "Let Vanessa explain it."

With great reluctance Leigh sat back down. "Talk, Vanessa. What's going on with this guy, and why are we just hearing about the dance part?"

"It's not like it sounds." Vanessa laughed again. Leigh never changed. "Ben collects antiques for his store. He's spending the week in Columbus looking for vintage goods."

"By himself?" Leigh's list of questions was ready to go. "Or are you doing a week of antiquing with him?"

"I'll help him find a few treasures . . . and he'll help me collect donations for the military family baskets."

"Sounds like fun." Maria smiled at her. "Romantic."

"It's like our own love story playing out here in the streets of Columbus." Leigh sat back in her chair and ate another few cashews. "And how am I just finding out about this?"

Vanessa held up her hand. "It's not like that. Ben and I are friends. That's all."

Leigh did a slow nod. Then she pointed her next cashew in Vanessa's direction. "And what does Sadie think of this *friend*?"

No easy answer came from Vanessa. Instead, the room fell silent and both Leigh and Maria turned to her. "You have told Sadie, right?" Maria looked concerned.

"I think the question is, 'Why haven't you told Sadie?'" Leigh shrugged. "Am I right?"

Deep breath, Vanessa told herself. She'd been asking herself the same question for weeks. "Like I said, it's not romantic. We're just friends."

"But Sadie doesn't know." Leigh shook her head and ate another few cashews. "Sounds like forbidden love to me."

The conversation went on that way for another few minutes until Vanessa had to leave. She assured her friends she'd keep them in the loop. "I'll introduce you to him tomorrow at church."

"By then Sadie has to know." Leigh blinked in Vanessa's direction. "A little hard to explain why some guy is hanging at your side all Sunday without saying something."

"Yes, Leigh." Vanessa ushered her friends to the door. "By then, Sadie will know."

Neither Leigh nor Maria asked, but as Vanessa drove the fifteen minutes to Old Town Columbus, she replayed the truth. She *had* tried to tell Sadie about Ben, but always Sadie was busy with her roommates or planning a study hall, headed to class or getting to sleep early for a big exam.

So the question wasn't whether she would tell Sadie about her friendship with Ben. Of course she would. The question was when.

Vanessa was parking near the RiverWalk and the outdoor Christmas Bazaar when her phone rang. She didn't recognize the number but she answered anyway, a habit she'd picked up since losing her Christmas ring.

"Hello?" Vanessa was in a hurry. Ben had already texted that he was walking the pathway, checking out the booths. Nothing came from the person on the other end of the call. "You must have the wrong—"

"Is this Vanessa Mayfield?" The voice was that of a younger man.

"Yes. How can I help you?" Vanessa was about to hang up when the man coughed a few times.

"Sorry... allergies." He sniffed. "Hey, so I think I found your ring. The one with the red ruby and the diamonds."

Vanessa released the grip she had on the steering wheel. "Where did you find it?"

"I'm Isaac Baker. I work at an antique shop outside Denver."

Vanessa's heart skipped a beat. "Colorado?"

"Yep. We're always sending out boxes of antiques that don't sell. I remember seeing that ring in a box we mailed out a week or so ago. Then today I found your flyer. Must've been in our back room for years."

Vanessa forced herself to focus. Their last trip to Colorado had been a few years ago. They'd had time before their flight, so she and Sadie had passed out flyers to antique stores near the airport. It was the last time they'd done that together.

"So... if it *was* my ring in the box, you're saying you don't actually have it?"

"I don't." Isaac explained that he had been trying to go through a list of stores where he might have sent the box with the ring. Unfortunately, he told Vanessa he had probably sent out fifty boxes of antiques in the past week. "I have a lot of tracking to do."

"I see." Vanessa waited. People who checked in with her about her missing ring almost always had a motive.

"What I wondered," Isaac continued, hesitating, "was whether the reward was still good. Otherwise there's no point in trying to find which store might have the box."

There it is. Vanessa slipped her keys into her purse. "The reward is still good. You can reach me at this number if you find it."

The call ended and Vanessa started toward the Christmas Bazaar. Isaac Baker might be legit. And maybe the ring he'd shipped off *had* been hers. It was the best lead she'd had in a year at least. But with the reward on the line, Vanessa had her doubts.

She spotted Ben before he saw her. He was looking at a booth of old books, talking to a couple who had brought their wares to the yearly bazaar. A rush of recent memories came to mind. She and Ben had found time to talk nearly every day, and on Saturdays they talked while walking at their separate parks.

He had told her about his hobby of woodworking and how he loved his men's Bible study. A place where he could grow in his faith and enjoy an outlet other than what he shared with his dad. They shared a common loss, one that most people never knew in their early forties. Ben was funny and deep and a great listener. But there were still things she didn't know about him. Like how his wife had died or how he had survived the loss.

She hadn't shared that either. With their extended time together starting today, Vanessa had a feeling they'd find their way to those deeper places.

Even from a distance Vanessa could see Ben smile at the couple and shake the man's hand. Like he really cared about the pair.

Watching Ben from a distance was sort of fun. Vanessa slowed her pace. She and Ben had only been together in person a few times. And now she could see for herself that her memory didn't do him justice.

This new friend of hers was not only a head-turning kind of handsome.

He was kind.

Chapter 6

FROM THE MOMENT HE pulled into town, Ben loved Columbus, Georgia. Like his heart had belonged here way before he parked his truck near the Chattahoochee RiverWalk. Christmas trees stood outside storefronts, decorating the coffeehouses and festive boutiques that marked the main road into Old Town, and American flags flew from half the houses.

The sense of military pride, patriotism, and Americana felt woven into the fabric of the buildings and people.

Columbus was bigger than Marietta, but something about it felt small. Like home. Vanessa had told him all the city's traditions: the annual lighting of the city Christmas tree in Old Town Square, dazzling light displays, and the Gingerbread Village where locals displayed original gingerbread houses to a growing crowd of visitors.

Then there was the RiverWalk Christmas Bazaar happening this weekend. Between this display of crafts and old heirlooms and the antique stores in town, there couldn't be a better time to search Columbus for unforgettable vintage Christmas goods.

His father had agreed, but he had also known Vanessa Mayfield lived here. "Take your time, son," he had told Ben when he left the store earlier today. "Treasures are rare and never easy to find."

Ben loved that his dad was a poet at heart. The two longed for the deeper things, and in fact his dad had first taught him about Walt Whitman. Ben played down his interest in Vanessa to his dad—and sometimes even to himself. In case nothing came of it. The two were only friends, after all. But there was no way he would be here looking for antiques in December except for one thing.

Vanessa lived here.

He breathed in deep, savoring the cool air off the river. Vanessa Mayfield had worked her way into his heart from the beginning. After losing Laura, he had never really expected to find love again. Most people didn't find a heart connection like that ever, let alone twice. But his conversations with Vanessa had been marked with familiarity from the beginning.

The other day he told the guys in his Bible study group about Vanessa and the trip to Columbus. Their consensus was the same. With God, to love again was possible. One of them put it succinctly: "It's about time, Ben."

He thought about her in the woodshop behind his house, the place where he processed his feelings and made rocking chairs that sold in the shop—the only non-antiques. She was on his mind when he worked out and when he drove to work and every Sunday when he fixed dinner for his dad and Gary and himself. Also, when the three of them played cornhole after eating.

The truth was, after just five months, Ben couldn't stop

thinking about her. And now as he walked along the waterside, he could practically feel Vanessa's warm and beautiful heart in the very air he was breathing.

He moseyed along the RiverWalk, eyeing the cold water and looking at one booth after another until he saw her. The wind played in her chestnut hair, and her amber eyes locked on his. In a single heartbeat her smile lit up the afternoon. Ben walked toward her as she made her way through the meandering crowd.

No matter what they called this connection they'd found, Ben was sure of one thing. He did not see her as merely a friend. But how did she feel about him? And was she ready for something that—with every passing week—felt like much more than friendship?

When they reached each other, they shared a quick hug. Vanessa was always careful not to linger, another reason Ben wasn't sure how she felt about him. But if her smile counted for anything, the possibility of something more certainly existed.

"So what do you think?" She wore a lightweight coat and a scarf and so did he. The weather was colder than usual, and the breeze off the river made it chillier.

"About Columbus? I love it." He broke away from her eyes to study the winding pathway and the river beyond it. "A Christmas bazaar along the RiverWalk? Brilliant."

They took their time, the breeze on their faces. The next booth held a table full of Christmas antiques. Exactly what Ben was looking for—workwise, anyway. They stopped and Ben sorted through the items. His eye caught a gold-plated bell. "I like it."

"So pretty." Vanessa ran her finger over the year engraved across the front. "Seventeen twelve."

"Okay. So here's the game." Ben could feel his eyes light up. He turned to Vanessa. "You hold the antique and get a feel for it. Then you let the story come to life."

"The story, huh." She leaned in, studying the bell. "Tell me."

Ben turned the bell over in his hands. "In the summer of 1718, a ship set sail from London headed to New York City. The vessel survived the journey, where many did not."

"Gripping." Vanessa faced him, hanging on every word. She was clearly having fun with the process.

"The reason?" Ben held up the antique. "One sailor held on to this very bell. When storms came, he would ring the bell. Sailors and passengers would take shelter . . . and survive. All because of the sound of the bell."

Ben rang the bell. The timbre was something no one could manufacture today. "This very bell."

The seller at the booth was eating a sandwich. He rolled his eyes. Antiques were apparently not his thing. Vanessa didn't seem to notice.

"Hmm." She pointed to a few scratches on the bell. "What about this? A lot of history here."

"Yes. I forgot that part." He shot Vanessa a smile and turned to the bell again. "At times, the sailor would fall across the slippery deck, just slide right across it. And the bell would fly from his hand. Terrible, really." Ben dropped his voice. "Hence the scratches."

Vanessa released a quiet laugh. "The sailor was a hero."

"And by default, so was the bell." Ben turned to the seller. "How much for this fine antique, my man?"

"Ten bucks." The guy had no sense of humor. "Firm."

"Very well." Ben pulled a ten from his wallet and handed it over. "The bell of the bazaar is mine."

The guy looked like he was maybe doing someone a favor working the booth. He wrapped the bell in a page of newspaper and slipped it into a bag. "Here you go." He handed the bag to Ben. "Unless you have another story in you."

Ben smiled at the guy. "You from Columbus?"

"Atlanta."

"I had a feeling." Ben saluted the seller. "Merry Christmas."

"Yeah, yeah." The man returned to his sandwich.

When they were out of earshot, Ben took a deep breath. "No way the guy was from Columbus."

Vanessa grinned. "No way."

An army convoy passed by, each of the trucks bearing a wreath on the front grill. Ben chuckled. "Tell me I'm not in a movie."

"You're not in a movie." Her arm brushed against his. "Columbus is always like this."

"All this time?" He met her eyes. "Look at what I've been missing."

They kept walking and Ben told her about December back in Marietta. "Christmas brings out the character in my hometown." He slid his hands into his pockets. "For instance... the mayor stopped by the other day."

"The mayor?" Vanessa looked confused.

"Yes. He walked through the door, his face covered entirely with gold paint."

"Gold?" Vanessa covered a laugh. "Is that... normal for your mayor?"

"Not exactly." Ben explained how the mayor shopped like that until he caught his reflection in the mirror. "Immediately he gasped. I thought he might faint right there on the floor of Millers' Antiques."

"So why was he out like that?" Vanessa slowed her pace, hanging on every word of the story.

"Turns out he was on a break from choir rehearsal at the church down the street. They're doing a Living Christmas Tree performance. And . . . the mayor is the star."

Vanessa couldn't contain her laugh this time. "Of course he's the star. He's the mayor."

"Next . . . six guys dressed like branches walked in. The first one came up to me and asked if we had any antique Christmas trees." Ben took a deep breath. "I told them maybe if they stood a little closer together they could—"

"Be the tree?"

"Just . . . you know." He motioned like he was bunching the branches together. "Be the tree. Exactly."

They started walking again and she narrowed her eyes. "Did that really happen?"

"Okay, no. I made that one up."

She laughed again and Ben found another funny story from the past week and then another and another.

Toward the end of the RiverWalk, Vanessa told him about Isaac Baker, the antique dealer who had called about her ring. "I doubt anything will come from it."

"I don't know." Ben stopped and faced her. "He has the picture, so this time the ring might really be yours."

She explained that the guy had a lot of tracing to do to even find the store where he'd sold the ring. If indeed it was her ring. "I'll see what he comes up with. I'm still praying I'll find it. Like Sadie and I would say back when I lost the ring, God knows where it is. He'll bring it back to me in His timing. If that's His will."

Ben searched her face, her eyes. "Great attitude." He sauntered beside her. "We both know that God doesn't always answer our prayers with a yes."

"He doesn't."

"But that was true for Jesus, too. His greatest prayer in the garden of Gethsemane was met with a 'no.'"

"Wow." Vanessa looked straight ahead for a moment. "I never thought of that."

They kept walking. The next table of vintage objects had a large gold star at the center. Ben picked it up and held it over his head. "For the mayor?"

More laughter. When they finished at the bazaar, they left her car and drove in his truck to pick up donations for the dance. Ben loved having her in his truck, riding shotgun next to him. Like the two had known each other for years.

She told him how the dance had helped fifty families survive Christmas last year and how this year they had a hundred on the list. "I think we can do it. The news is running a piece about the fundraiser, and the community is more aware. Everyone wants to help."

Ben glanced at her. "Now I'm impressed." Their eyes held. "Since the day I met you."

Her eyes were more locked in, their connection stronger. She smiled, demure. "Thank you."

Their first stop was the candy store. Mrs. Benson was

one of the supporters of Columbus Cares, and she had offered to donate a hundred chocolate Christmas trees for the family baskets.

They walked inside the shop and Ben stopped. He'd never seen anything like the place. Candy covered every inch. All around him were shelves of it, rows and displays and boxes of it. "You know." He leaned close and whispered to Vanessa, "I was really hoping I could find some candy in this place."

Vanessa giggled. "Stop."

Mrs. Benson finished up with a customer. When the patron left, she turned to Ben and Vanessa. "Well, hello there." The shopkeeper eyed Ben. "And who may I ask is this?"

"This is my friend. Ben Miller." Vanessa tried to keep a straight face. Her cheeks were already pink, likely from the woman's reaction. "Ben, this is Margaret Benson. Everyone's favorite grandmother."

"And candy lady!" Mrs. Benson gave Ben a thumbs-up. The woman was in her late seventies, Vanessa had told him. But she had the spunk of someone half her age. Ben had to agree.

Mrs. Benson walked out from behind the counter and pointed to a large bag on the floor in front of the register. "There they are—a hundred chocolate Christmas trees."

Vanessa took Mrs. Benson's hand and gave it a gentle squeeze. "You're amazing. Thank you." Vanessa started for the bag, but Ben got there first.

"I'll carry them." He grinned at her.

"Vanessa Mayfield." Mrs. Benson put her hands on her hips. "Don't you tell me that handsome man is just a friend. You two better figure it out."

Nice, Ben thought to himself. He wanted to thank the older woman for saying so, but instead he only smiled at her. "Nice meeting you."

"Yes, thank you again, Mrs. Benson." Vanessa gave her a smile and a slight shake of her head.

Mrs. Benson seemed to get the hint. She gave a light shrug. "Just saying, Vanessa."

When Ben and Vanessa stepped outside, Ben chuckled. "I think I like her."

"Sorry." Vanessa covered her face with one hand. She was laughing again. "Mrs. Benson doesn't hold back."

They walked past a few antique shops. "They're on my list for tomorrow. After church." Vanessa pulled a piece of paper from her purse. "Here. It's all the antique shops in Columbus worth visiting."

Ben glanced at the list and his heart melted a little more. "You didn't have to do that."

"I figured that way you wouldn't waste your time here."

Their arms brushed together again, and Ben wanted only to make the afternoon stop, to take her in his arms and look long into her eyes. Instead, he studied the list again and slipped it into his coat pocket.

Vanessa needed to get back, so he drove her to her car. Before she stepped out he turned to her. "When does Sadie get in?"

"Seven o'clock. I'm making her favorite lasagna for dinner."

"She should come with us tomorrow." Ben was under no delusions about the situation with Sadie. There would be no future with Vanessa unless Sadie approved.

"Ben." Vanessa stopped and faced him. "She doesn't know about you yet. About us. Being friends."

A shiver of concern passed through Ben, but he didn't let it show. "I thought you told her."

"I wanted to. I . . . I think I'm supposed to tell her in person."

"Okay." He smiled, his expression easy. "But you'll tell her? Tonight?"

"That's my plan."

"Good." Ben didn't want to make an issue out of it. "We're still on for church tomorrow?"

"Nine o'clock service." Her smile looked as sincere as before. Nothing had changed, despite the bumpy bit about Sadie. She raised her brow. "Oh, and park out back."

They both climbed out of his truck and walked to her car. Ben helped get her bags in the back seat, then he hugged her. The way he'd been longing to do since the embrace that started today's adventures. Again, he kept it quick. He brushed her hair from her eyes. "I had fun today."

"A lot better than FaceTime." She put her hand alongside his face, and for a moment it seemed neither of them wanted to break away.

But it was too soon for more, so Ben was the first to take a step back. "Okay, then. See you tomorrow."

"See you, Ben." Vanessa smiled once more, then climbed into her car.

He leaned against his truck and watched her drive away.

The entire day was like a dream. And as he got back behind the wheel, he smiled to himself. God was up to something, he could tell. Because for the first time since losing Laura, Ben felt ready to move on. Whatever God was doing in his heart, as he drove to his hotel, Ben had one word to describe the way he felt about Vanessa Mayfield.

Smitten.

THE OLD, dusty antique shop was quiet, the customers long gone for the day. Not that the man had been able to focus on making sales. Hardly. All he could think about was the beautiful ring, the one that had come in a box of mixed heirlooms and aging pieces.

Now the box was down on the floor, and the ring sat perched in a small cardboard box in front of him. The man couldn't tell for sure, but he had a hunch about this one. After so many years working with antiques, replicas, and genuine treasures, he had a feeling this one was real. He had paid fifty dollars for the box of goods with no guarantees about what it held.

This was the way he and most of his peers did business. Because with antiques, the value was in the eye of the customer. And no one knew the customers better than the antique dealers at each store. Some shops specialized in old books or machinery, pens or dishes. Others did not. Pretty straightforward.

Unless, of course, a man like him might stumble onto something real. He studied the ring again. The dark gold band and ruby-red stone surrounded by that pretty ring of shimmery diamonds. Yes, he definitely had a suspicion about this one.

He would get it appraised. That would tell him the actual story. But if he had to guess, he would bet everything in his store that this one, this beautiful ring, was not a replica.

It was real. As real as Christmas itself.

Chapter 7

THE HOUSE SMELLED LIKE lasagna and already Sadie had called twice to say she was on time and excited to be home. Even though dinner was just for the two of them, Vanessa had decorated the table and set out her special Christmas china plates and serving dishes.

Sadie had been home briefly for Thanksgiving. The dinner had been with Leigh and Maria and their kids, and the time had gone by in a flash. Christmas break would give Vanessa more time to reconnect with her daughter.

Sadie was halfway through her first year and Christmas was a week away! They had every reason to celebrate!

Of course, maybe just the tiniest part of all of this was to help Sadie feel comfortable when Vanessa broke the news about Ben. An atmosphere to remind her daughter that nothing would ever change between them. Even if Vanessa did have a new friend.

She tried to imagine how difficult the past five months would have been if she hadn't had the delightful distraction of Ben Miller. A smile came over her. Ben had been just what she needed.

Vanessa made a quick assessment of tonight's welcome home dinner for Sadie, and she nodded. Everything was in order. Lasagna and garlic bread were warm in the oven, the salad freshly tossed with Sadie's favorite balsamic vinaigrette dressing. An iced bottle of Gerolsteiner sparkling water sat in the middle of the table. Sadie's favorite.

Vanessa stared at the clear glass bottle. She could still hear Alan's voice. *"If it's Sadie we're celebrating, get that fancy water. The one I can never pronounce."* Some days it was still hard to believe he would never walk through the door again, never celebrate with them each birthday and Christmas. Maybe even crazier was the fact that today, while she was out with Ben, she hadn't thought once about Alan.

She looked at her wedding ring and felt the hint of tears. Time was moving her away from those days. Giving her a second chance at life, which was something she had prayed for. But now that it was happening, her sadness shifted. Not that she couldn't stop thinking about Alan.

But today, for the first time, she had.

With everything set, Vanessa wandered into Sadie's room. The place was just how she'd left it, her bed made, closet neatly put together. Her desk intact with a dozen small framed photos of her high school days and family moments before Alan had died. And of course pictures of her and Hudson. Vanessa smiled. Sadie was going to love Ben. It was just a matter of time.

Something on the floor behind Sadie's headboard caught Vanessa's eye, and she moved closer to see what it was. She bent down and picked it up as an ache filled her heart. It was Sadie's little brown bear, the one she'd had since she was in kindergarten.

Vanessa stared at the bear. She'd been in Sadie's room during the past few months to vacuum, but somehow she'd missed this. She stroked the little bear's head. Normally it sat up on Sadie's pillow, where it had sat until she left for college.

Mister Bear was the one thing Sadie had always held on to when she fell asleep.

But obviously Sadie had left it here when she moved to Reinhardt.

Vanessa picked up the bear, dusted it off, and set it back on Sadie's pillow. "There." She patted the little bear. "Sadie will be glad we found you."

She heard a sound at the front door and hurried out of Sadie's room to see her daughter drag a suitcase and two bags into the house. "Sadie!"

"Mom!" She left her things and ran into Vanessa's arms. "I missed you so much."

"Sadie girl. You're home." The feel of her daughter in her arms, the smell of her blonde hair and freshly washed clothes. Her little girl was home, and this time Vanessa couldn't stop the emotion welling inside her. "It's so good to see you."

Once during the semester, Vanessa had visited Sadie at Reinhardt, and the two had shared lunch. It was one of the times she had spent the afternoon shopping with Ben. Now that her daughter was home, Vanessa definitely felt guilty for not mentioning Ben before. She should have.

Vanessa studied her. "You look beautiful. School agrees with you."

"I had to figure it out." Sadie's laugh sounded light and carefree. "After the first week it was sort of sink or swim." She grabbed her bags and pulled them toward the hallway. "You know what Dad always said. 'There's no sinking in this family. Better find your flippers.'"

"Yes." Vanessa smiled. "I remember." Alan had been full of comments like that, words of wisdom that stayed with her and Sadie and would continue to stay as long as they lived.

Vanessa helped Sadie put her things away. Then they filled their plates and sat at the table. Sadie ran her fingertips over the fancy lace cloth. "You didn't have to do all this, Mom."

"My daughter comes home from college for the first time ever?" Vanessa grinned. "I stopped short of getting a marching band and a balloon arch, but this?" She looked at the table. "This was the least I could do."

Vanessa prayed over the meal, asking God to bless their time together and the upcoming dance. As soon as they said, "Amen," Vanessa's questions bubbled to the surface. "Did you take all your finals?"

"I did." Sadie took another bite of lasagna. "Mom, this might be your best ever."

"Thank you." She was glad Sadie had noticed. "The noodles are homemade."

"Wow! You must've been working in the kitchen all day."

"Yes, well." A single laugh came from Vanessa. "Not *all*

day. We had the volunteer brunch this morning. Everyone's getting ready for the dance." Was this the right time to tell Sadie? Vanessa set down her fork. "Also, after the brunch—"

"The dance is going to be amazing, Mom! I still hope Hudson can come."

"Right." Vanessa felt the moment pass. "What about your grades, honey? Have you seen anything from your tests or papers?"

"It all looks good so far." Sadie's smile looked a bit more forced.

"You have to watch it because sometimes they enter the wrong grade. Then you have to fight the process and get them to make the changes before too much time lapses." Vanessa took a quick breath. "Otherwise, they'll refuse to go back and correct the mistake and—"

"Mom." Sadie held up her hand. Her smile told Vanessa she was done talking about this. "I know all that. I'm trying to be an adult, like you and Dad taught me." Sadie seemed to remember her smile. "I know you're just trying to help, but everything is okay with my grades." She took another bite. "What about you? What else have you been up to?"

This was her chance. "Funny you should ask."

Just then Sadie's phone rang. She checked the caller ID and grinned at Vanessa. "It's Ella. I need to take it." Sadie dropped her voice to a whisper. "Trouble with her boyfriend. I'll be right back."

And just like that, Sadie hurried away from the table and down the hall to her bedroom. Vanessa could hear her chatting as she ran out of sight. She studied the table. Sadie had almost finished her dinner. No telling how long she would talk to Hudson's sister. They probably had a ton to catch up on.

Vanessa cleared the table and leaned against the counter. She had to tell Sadie about Ben before tomorrow. Like her friends had pointed out earlier today, she could hardly walk into church at Ben's side without telling Sadie something.

Or could she?

SADIE NEVER normally felt strained around her mother. What was the feeling—scrutiny or mistrust? Like her mom didn't think she had her life together? Whatever it was, Sadie wanted things between them back to normal.

Twenty minutes into the call with Ella, Sadie got a text from Hudson. She grinned. "Your brother wants to FaceTime me." She hesitated. "I'm still hoping he'll be here for the dance."

"I wouldn't count on it." Ella sighed. "My mom told me yesterday. Hudson's unit has to stay through Christmas."

"We'll see." Sadie could hardly wait to talk to Hudson. "I gotta go. Let's get together tomorrow after church."

The call with Ella ended and Sadie positioned her laptop on her desk. She flipped on her small ring light and waited for Hudson's call to come through. Service from the Middle East wasn't always great, but usually they could talk five or ten minutes before he had to go or the signal died.

A minute later Sadie's screen lit up. In a blink she and Hudson were looking at each other face-to-face. As if he wasn't a million miles away with his life on the line. One of Fort Benning's army Rangers.

"Hi." His smile melted her heart. "I've been thinking about you all afternoon."

"Me, too." She raked her fingers through her hair. "What'd you do today?" She didn't expect an answer. Special Operations Forces couldn't tell family and friends much about what they did with their time.

"Patrolled." He looked tired. "The usual. Did you get your grades?"

"I got A's in everything but child development." Sadie made a sad face. "And you already know how I feel about that."

"My girlfriend's about to be anything but an education major." He chuckled. "You have to tell your mom."

"I know. Maybe tomorrow." Sadie rested her head on her hand. "How do you think she'll handle it?"

"I mean, you've only wanted to be a teacher since you were, what, in first grade?" Hudson chuckled again, but he wasn't really laughing. "No, really. I think she'll be okay. That's what college is for, right? Figuring it out."

Sadie thought about it. Hudson was right. Her mother wouldn't be mad. They would talk about it and she would understand how dreams change and directions shift. Surely.

"Hey, Rogers." The voice from off-screen boomed. "Briefing's in five minutes."

Hudson looked toward the voice. "I'll be there." After a beat he looked back at Sadie. "I have to go. It's never enough."

"No." Sadie remembered what Ella said. "I talked to your sister. She said you aren't coming home for Christmas."

A sigh came from deep inside Hudson. Clearly this wasn't easy for him. "I'm not. We found out yesterday." All humor faded from his expression. "I asked around, but it's for sure. No one goes home this Christmas. Things are tense." He looked like he wanted to say more, but he couldn't.

"Got it." Sadie understood. "No dance for you and me."

"Not this year." He put his hand on the computer screen and she did the same, their hands touching through the Internet connection. "You sure you wanna do this, Sadie Mayfield? Date an army Ranger?"

"Yes." She didn't hesitate. "I knew what I was getting into when you asked me on that first date." She paused and allowed herself to get lost in his eyes. "It won't always be like this."

"Rogers, let's go!" This time the voice barked the order.

"Gotta run." Hudson held her eyes a moment longer. "Bye, Sadie."

"Bye. I'm praying for you. Every day."

Before Hudson could thank her or tell her he loved her, before she could say the same thing, the screen went black. Which was pretty much how their calls always ended. Army Rangers had little time to themselves while they were deployed. She thought about her dad and his buddies, the men and women from Fort Benning who gave up everything to keep the country safe. No, the heavy demands of Hudson's job didn't bother Sadie.

They only made her love him more.

Chapter 8

FROM THE BEGINNING, SUNDAY went nothing like Vanessa had planned. For starters, Sadie was still sound asleep as Vanessa got ready. She thought about waking her, but Sadie had been up late talking to Ella. After a week of finals, most college kids needed a little extra rest.

Vanessa made the drive to church alone, and as she did she thought about Sadie's first night home. There had only been half an hour where she and Sadie could talk. They had stood near the Christmas tree so Sadie could hang her favorite photo ornament—the one of Vanessa and Alan and Sadie when she was in eighth grade.

Their last formal picture as a family.

The whole time Vanessa had looked for a way to tell Sadie about Ben. Vanessa could've been wrong, but she wondered if maybe Sadie had wanted to talk about something, too. In the end, neither of them got that far.

The problem was simple. Vanessa wasn't the only person glad to have Sadie home. Finally, when Sadie turned in last night, Vanessa figured she would simply introduce Sadie to Ben at church. Keep things casual.

But she was still asleep when Vanessa walked out the door.

Instead of having Sadie with her, Sunday service that morning turned out to be the place where Vanessa introduced Ben to Maria and Leigh. The two practically ran up when Vanessa and Ben entered the back of the church.

Leigh didn't even try to keep her voice down. "You must be Ben Miller." She held out her hand and shook his. She didn't wait for a response. "I'm Leigh." She elbowed their other friend. "This is Maria."

Maria didn't try to interject. She merely raised her hand and smiled. Vanessa hung her head for a moment and then looked up, laughing. There was no stopping Leigh.

Ben seized the break from Leigh. He smiled at Vanessa's friends. "Nice to meet you both."

Leigh pointed to herself, Maria, and Vanessa. "We're a trio. With Vanessa, that is. Not a singing trio. We aren't touring. Just a trio. Of friends."

"Ah yes. The dance committee." Ben rolled with Leigh's antics. His charming attitude only made Vanessa more attracted to him.

"That's us." Leigh smiled, obviously proud of herself.

Maria cut in. "We've been friends since we met." She smiled at Leigh, then Vanessa. "We have a lot in common, don't we, girls?"

Vanessa loved these friends of hers. They were genuine through and through.

A cool breeze came over the grassy front yard of the church. Maria turned to Vanessa. "Where's Sadie?"

"She needed her sleep. She was wiped." Vanessa felt her phone buzz. She checked it. "This is her! We're going to meet up back at the house after the service."

"I remember my first semester of college." Ben seemed careful not to stand too close to Vanessa. He glanced at Maria and Leigh. "I'd come home and sleep fifteen hours straight."

"That happened to me, too. In fact, it still does." Leigh shook her head. "And I never even took a class."

The group laughed and found their seats. Maria and Leigh sat at the end of the same pew. Vanessa couldn't exactly hear them, but her two friends might as well have been shouting the obvious. Vanessa could see it in their raised eyebrows when Ben wasn't looking.

They clearly thought something was going on.

The sermon was like it was written for Vanessa and Ben. The focus was on Joseph and how he kept moving forward. He didn't look back and get lost in the past. If he hadn't listened to God and kept moving ahead, what would've happened? There would've been no Mary and Joseph, and without her husband, how would Mary have survived?

Joseph obeyed God and did the next thing even when it was difficult. And as a result, the Savior was born and the world was changed.

When the service was over, Maria and Leigh approached. After a few minutes of talk about the service, Maria took a step back.

"Well, on that note, Leigh and I need to go chat about tomorrow's Gingerbread House Competition."

Vanessa grinned at Ben. "Another highlight for Columbus Cares. We started it last year for the kids of deployed soldiers."

Leigh shook her head. "This year will be a doozy. We have about a dump truck of icing."

"Last year, most of it wound up on the parking lot asphalt." Maria wiped the back of her hand across her forehead at the memory. "Talk about a mess. It was everywhere. Kids had sticky tennis shoes till spring."

Ben chuckled. "Sounds like a good time."

"Yeah. That's it!" Leigh nodded at Vanessa. "You should bring him by."

"Actually . . ." Vanessa shook her head. "We have plans. Ben has work to do."

Maria raised her eyebrows. "Okay, then. I guess we'll be on our way."

The two left and Vanessa and Ben walked toward the parking lot. Again, Ben seemed to be careful. He didn't walk too close or let his gaze linger. As if he knew well the fact that Maria and Leigh and many of Vanessa's friends were probably watching them.

As they reached her car, Ben was still talking about the pastor's words. "It made me think." He stopped and smiled at her.

The sun was bright that morning, the air still chilly. Vanessa shaded her eyes. "Me, too. The importance of not getting lost in the past." She had felt that deeply. The words applied to them both.

"Joseph knew when to let go of all that had shaped his

life . . . and when to look ahead. At things seen only in visions of angels." Ben cocked his head. "Profound."

"Mmm." Vanessa could feel him working his way into her heart. "Old Walt would be proud."

"Thank you." Ben chuckled. "I'll take that as a compliment."

Ben had to connect with his dad about work, and Vanessa needed to get home to Sadie. They agreed to meet at the Perfect Find at three. "And this time bring Sadie." Ben grinned. "If she wants to join us."

"I will." Vanessa hesitated. "I'll see." Vanessa waved and climbed into her SUV.

Almost immediately Ben pulled out his phone. Vanessa could see him standing outside his truck, face to the sun as he made the call. He waved as she drove out of sight, and only then did Vanessa exhale. Every moment with Ben was better than the last. Friendship or whatever, she wasn't just having a great visit with Ben.

She was falling for him.

BEN HAD a few reasons he needed to talk to his father that Sunday afternoon. He had planned to go home for a day before the dance, but now he didn't want to leave. He couldn't imagine missing out on the chance to spend the whole week in Columbus.

The store was closed on Sundays, but his dad and Gary often stopped by after church to unload boxes and play a game of chess. His dad picked up on the first ring.

"Ben, my boy, good to hear from you." His dad's voice was chipper. Christmas music played in the background. Something from Frank Sinatra.

"Happy Sunday, Dad. How was church?" Ben kept his face to the sun. The warmth felt good after so many cold days.

"Wonderful. Talked about the wise men." His dad mumbled something to Gary.

In the background, Ben heard Gary complaining. "Tell your dad he can't move his rook right out the gate. It's bad manners!"

Ben laughed. "Hey, Dad, listen, I have a question. What would you think about me staying in Columbus until Christmas Eve? The day after Vanessa's big dance?"

"Christmas Eve?" Ben's father seemed surprised by the idea. "What about all the treasures you're buying? We should get them into the storefront. Last-minute shoppers need fresh merchandise."

Ben thought his dad might say that. "What about the boxes? Anything new there?"

"Gary and I went through them. The folks around here buy up our best stuff before we can open the next container. You know how it goes."

Ben was careful to hide his disappointment. His dad deserved better. "Okay, then, let's say I come back on Tuesday night. We can set out what I find here and I'll head back on Thursday morning so we can look around some more."

"I like that." His father seemed to take his time. "How was your service?"

Ben smiled. "It was about Joseph."

"Now there's a man who loved his wife."

Ben closed his eyes and tried to picture Joseph. "He would've done anything for her."

"That's how I felt about your mother." The chess game was obviously forgotten for the moment. "How can this be so many Christmases without her?"

"I feel her with me." Ben paced a few steps away and then back to his truck. "I always will."

"And one of these days, I'll find that diamond in the rough, Ben. Then we can take that trip to Italy. Something she always wanted."

Ben loved his dad. Such a good heart. "It'll happen. One of these days."

Gary called out again, "Your turn, Howard. Let the young man go."

"I will." His dad's voice grew more thoughtful. "Who's we?"

"We?"

"Yes. We." His dad's tone was kind. "You said, 'So we can look around some more.' Who's we? The woman you've been talking with?"

"Yes. Her." Ben never held back with his dad. "To be honest, I may have found my own diamond in the rough. Mom would've loved her."

"Well"—his dad's smile sounded in his voice—"your mother always believed you'd find love again."

"I'm starting to believe that, too."

Cars were parking in the lot now, and what seemed like choir members began to stream into the church. Ben bid his father and Gary goodbye and hung up. All he wanted to do was surprise Vanessa and stop by her house. But if this was the time when she was going to talk to Sadie, then he couldn't interrupt them. His desire to be with her would have to wait.

Even so, three o'clock couldn't come fast enough.

VANESSA PICKED up two lattes from Harvest Coffee in Old Town and returned home in time to hear Sadie ending a FaceTime call with Hudson. Sadie's door was open, but Vanessa knocked on the doorframe anyway.

"Come in." Sadie closed her laptop, pushed back from her desk, and stood. She took one of the lattes. "So nice, Mom. Thank you."

The two hugged. "Your favorite." Vanessa sat with her coffee on the edge of Sadie's bed. "How's Hudson?"

"Tense again. I think they're in more danger." Sadie took a sip of her coffee. "No details of course."

"There never are." Vanessa studied Sadie. "Did you get enough rest?"

"Yes." Sadie looked slightly hurt. "How come you didn't wake me? I wanted to go."

"Aw, honey." Vanessa felt bad. "You looked so tired. I thought you could use the sleep."

A yawn came from Sadie. She laughed. "I guess I did."

They were quiet for a moment, sipping their lattes. Vanessa reached back and picked up Sadie's brown bear. "Did you mean to leave Mister Bear behind?"

Another light laugh came from Sadie. She patted the bear's head. "Cute little guy."

"Remember how you used to pray with him when he was scared? You'd say, 'Mister Bear is afraid of the dark. So I had to remind him about Jesus.' Then you'd hold him tight and say, 'He's going to be okay.'"

Sadie tilted her head, her eyes soft. "I remember."

"Sadie, I've been meaning to tell you about something. For the last—"

An alarm sounded from Sadie's phone. She gasped. "Can it wait, Mom? Classes are up!"

"Classes. For next semester?"

"Yes." Sadie hurried back to her desk chair and opened her laptop. "I can't wait."

Vanessa felt an ache in her gut. "I thought . . . I figured we would pick your classes together. While you were home."

"I had to pick them weeks ago." Sadie glanced back at her. "Didn't I tell you?"

"You didn't." Still holding the bear, Vanessa stood and moved behind her daughter. "Can I see?"

"Of course." Sadie signed into her college portal and pulled up her spring class list.

Vanessa scanned the courses. "Wait. Honey, you didn't get into early education. You need that for your teaching credential."

This seemed to hit Sadie. She pushed back from her desk and faced Vanessa again. "I was going to tell you yesterday." Sadie stood and reached for Vanessa's hand. "Mom . . . I'm not sure about teaching."

"What?" Vanessa felt the floor shift beneath her feet. "But you've always wanted to be a teacher. Ever since you were a little girl."

"Not anymore. I guess it took college for me to figure it out."

For a moment Vanessa imagined Alan coming home from the base, his medic patch on the sleeve of his uniform. "Your father taught the other medics and you . . . you always wanted to be just like him."

"But Mom . . . it's my future, right? I'll figure it out, but I don't want to be a teacher. That's what I wanted to tell you last night, but we ran out of time."

There was nothing wrong with Sadie's tone. The news was shocking, that's all. "Okay, sure. I mean, yes, it's your future." Vanessa felt the picture she'd always held of the future crumble a bit. "I just never dreamed . . ."

Vanessa was trying to figure out what else to say when Sadie's phone rang. She looked up. "It's Ella. I won't be long. I'm going to her house in an hour. They invited me for dinner!"

"Sure. Of course." Vanessa remembered to smile. "I'll be in the living room."

Already Sadie was into her other conversation. "You won't believe it! I got into photography!" Sadie sounded as thrilled as she did on Christmas morning. "Everyone said I wouldn't get that class till next year, but I'm in it!"

Vanessa waited a beat. Then she stood and placed Mister Bear back on the pillow at the head of Sadie's bed. She looked back at Sadie and a thought occurred to her. This was a different daughter than the one she'd taken to Breckenridge four years ago. Different from the one she'd dropped off at Reinhardt last July. Her daughter was growing up, and that wasn't a bad thing. Just different.

And something about that broke Vanessa's heart.

Chapter 9

BEN COULD TELL SOMETHING was off with Vanessa the minute they met up at the Perfect Find. She hugged him, maybe a little longer than last time. But the light in her eyes wasn't as bright as before. He stayed there with her, in no hurry to get inside the shop.

"Everything okay?"

Vanessa sighed. "I'm fine. It's Sadie. She's just . . . older, I guess. Things between us feel different." She smiled, even if it didn't quite reach her eyes. She told Ben about Sadie no longer wanting to be a teacher and how she'd chosen classes without Vanessa's help.

He and Laura had never had children, but he felt for her. "You pray for them to find their way . . . and then when they do, it can't be easy."

"It isn't." Vanessa's laugh sounded heavy. "We'll be okay. She's only been home a day. We just need time. And right now she's at her friend's house."

"You're right. You need time. That's all." Ben opened the door for her and they stepped inside. The place gave Millers' Antiques a run for its money when it came to

Christmas décor. That much was obvious even from the entrance.

Ben noticed an arrow and a sign: *Mistletoe Section this way.*

He grinned. "Apparently they have a mistletoe section." He tried not to look at Vanessa too long. *Friends. She only wants to be friends.*

Even so, they walked to the mistletoe room first. Ben looked around as they entered. "I'll say this for the owners. They're serious about their mistletoe."

There were mistletoe ornaments and wall hangings and ribbons and dishes. Salt and pepper shakers and socks. Everything mistletoe including, well, actual mistletoe.

"Hmm." Vanessa giggled. Already her mood seemed lighter. "You have to wonder, right?"

Ben gave her the flirtiest look he would allow. "I mean . . . I get it."

She laughed, her cheeks a bit redder.

Their look held. Ben glanced up and sure enough, mistletoe hung overhead. They both laughed this time and moved into the next section of the store. The kindling of their chemistry had been there from the beginning.

But now it seemed to ignite.

They moved to a Christmassy bookcase. Antiques had a way of stirring Ben's heart, taking him to the places of poetry in his soul. He took a fountain pen from one of the shelves. "Who owned it?" He turned his eyes to Vanessa again. "What letters did that person write? What thoughts poured from his heart?"

"Okay." Vanessa clearly loved this. "I can play." She

took the pen and turned it over in her hand. "She was a playwright, longing for her big break. Then one night she wrote a story that would change her life. And that one story caught the eye of a producer, who fell in love with her words. And in turn, he fell in love with her."

She understood the game. Ben loved that about her. "Perfection." Ben took the pen again. "Antiques let you hold a piece of history in your hand."

"And wonder about the person who held it first." Vanessa seemed to glance at her wedding ring. "The one no longer here this Christmas."

Ben wanted to take her hand, wanted to pull her close. But he waited. Giving her space was the best way he knew to honor Vanessa and her feelings. Especially after she'd just looked at her wedding ring.

He smiled straight into her eyes. "The trick is knowing when to hold on to the past." He put the pen back on the bookshelf. "And when to let it go."

After they'd scoured the store, Ben bought several items including the fountain pen. It wasn't a Christmas item, but their customers were always looking for pens and paper and typewriters. Evidence that the deeper ways of communicating had always been around.

They stepped outside and Ben's phone rang. It was his dad.

"Let me get this." He motioned to Vanessa.

"I'll pick up the bag of teddy bears from two doors down." Vanessa motioned to the toy shop. "Let's meet back here."

Ben leaned against the old brick wall and watched her

go. She exuded life, and the spring in her step made her seem like a girl in her twenties. Just another thing Ben loved about her. He took the call. "Hey, Dad. What's up?"

"It happened!" His dad was always a happy man, but his tone was at an entirely different level. He was practically giddy and his words ran together. "I found it, Ben! The diamond in the rough!"

"Dad." Ben chuckled. He pressed the phone closer to his ear. "Slow down. I can't understand you."

"The diamond in the rough! I found it." His dad exhaled and found a more reasonable pace. "It was this pretty bauble stuck in a box of a hundred other antiques. I looked past it three times before it jumped out at me."

"It jumped out at you?" Ben tried to imagine exactly what type of bauble it must be.

"Not literally, son. But almost. Something about it made me want to get it appraised. Just in case. So I did, right after we talked earlier."

Ben smiled. "An appraisal is a good way to know." This was why he loved working with his dad. His enthusiasm knew no limits. "And?"

"Ben!" His father paused. "It appraised for twenty-five thousand dollars!"

Shock, like the December wind in southern Georgia that week, washed over Ben. "Dad . . . is this a Christmas joke?"

"No joke, son. This is real. As real as that appraisal."

Ben walked the length of the store and back again. "What are you going to do with it?"

"Sell it!" He laughed. "Ben, I have a buyer all lined up.

She'll be here the twenty-third." His dad let out a shout. "Merry Christmas to us both, my boy!"

The reality was settling in. "Looks like we'll be taking that trip to Italy after all."

"Better believe it!" His dad hooted once more. "Gary hasn't stood up since I told him. We're all in shock."

Ben saw Vanessa approach with two large bags. With every step she struggled to keep them off the ground for more than a few seconds.

"Hey, Dad. I have to go. Amazing news. I still can't believe it."

The call ended and Ben hurried to take the bags from Vanessa. She must have noticed something different about him. "You look happy."

"My dad found a valuable antique. He had it appraised." The wonder of it all came over Ben again.

Vanessa walked beside Ben now. "Worth a lot?"

"Yeah." Ben looked at her and their eyes held. For a moment he stopped and it was just him and Vanessa. "The find of a lifetime."

She clearly understood what he meant. He could tell by the way her eyes sparkled.

They were about to head across the street for coffee when Vanessa's phone rang. The call was quick but Vanessa looked concerned. When she hung up, she turned to Ben.

"Two volunteers dropped out of the Gingerbread House Contest. I need to reach out to a few people and get it covered."

Ben set the bags down and held out both arms. "Didn't I tell you? I love gingerbread houses! Let's do this."

"Really?" Vanessa laughed. "You amaze me."

They put the bags in her car and headed for the church. The contest was set up outside, apparently same as last year. As he and Vanessa walked up, the event was in full happy Christmassy chaos.

For the next hour, Ben worked alongside Vanessa helping kids frost their houses and find the right candy decorations.

When it was time for cleanup, Ben had an idea. He spoke so only Vanessa could hear him. "What if I read to the kids while you all clean up?"

A tenderness filled Vanessa's eyes. "They'd love that."

So Ben grabbed a Bible from inside the church and gathered the kids on the front steps. "My grandfather used to read this to me every Christmas."

He opened the Bible to Luke Two and began to read. The kids were quiet, holding onto every word. "But the angel said to them, 'Do not be afraid. I bring you good news that will cause great joy for all the people. Today in the town of David a Savior has been born to you; He is the Messiah, the Lord. This will be a sign to you: You will find a baby wrapped in cloths and lying in a manger. Suddenly a great company of the heavenly host appeared with the angel, praising God and saying, 'Glory to God in the highest heaven, and on earth peace to those on whom His favor rests.'"

A little boy stood up and smiled. "That's what Christmas is all about!"

The kids giggled, and just then Ben looked across the cleanup crew and saw Vanessa watching him. They both smiled and Ben felt a thrill of hope. Like Christmas itself.

Because her smile was far more than that of a friend.

Later Ben helped the team fold up the cleaned tables. One man and a little girl, maybe eight years old, were still there, talking off to one side of the parking lot. He was clearly remarking about her gingerbread house.

Vanessa saw him watching the two. "That's Lexi. She lost her mom overseas three months ago. Her dad told me this is the first time he's seen her smile since."

Ben felt his heart sink. The price for freedom was never free. Lexi and her father were proof.

He watched Vanessa folding up chairs a few feet away. She took this sort of thing in stride. This town was familiar with the very greatest loss, but they pushed through all the same. They stood by each other and believed in the job their family members signed up for.

And something about that made Ben care even more for Vanessa Mayfield.

VANESSA FELL for him a little more every time they were together. And today most of all. After finishing with the gingerbread house competition, they went to Harvest, the best coffee shop in Columbus. When they had their drinks, they took a table near the window. From there they could see the Christmas displays that lined the center of Old Town.

Ben leaned back in his chair. "So tell me more about Columbus Cares."

She realized again how much he cared about her, about the things she loved. They weren't in a hurry. The coffee shop would be open another two hours, so she took her time. She told him how Alan had always wanted to do something to help the local military families. "After he died, I had to do something. It just made sense to start Columbus Cares. By then I'd met Maria and Leigh."

"That Leigh is a hoot." Ben laughed. "But your trio doesn't tour. She was sure to tell me that."

"She's hilarious. Every time the trio gets together, Maria and I laugh till we cry." Vanessa thought back to their original meeting. "It's sort of incredible to think we met at a grief support group."

Vanessa told him how the meeting had been for Gold Star Widows.

"I didn't know." Ben seemed to take the news personally. "Maria and Leigh . . . ?"

"Yes. They both lost their husbands, too. Different attacks, but the same month."

Ben was quiet for a moment. "You don't realize the price. Going through life every day. The freedoms we have." He sighed. "Not until you hear something like this. The losses you've each suffered."

She appreciated his kindness, the way he genuinely seemed to understand and appreciate the military.

For a long moment they drank their coffees, letting the discussion have its space. "I think your dad is going to like the things you're finding."

Ben leaned forward after a beat, his elbows on the table. "You know, Vanessa." His voice was kind. "You change the subject whenever Alan comes up."

His words hit their mark. "I do. I'm sorry." Vanessa felt

tears form in her eyes, and she put her hand over her heart. "It's like he belongs here. In a place I can't let anyone in."

"I get that." Again, Ben didn't rush the moment. Something Vanessa was growing to appreciate more each time they were together. He set his coffee down. "Can you tell me about him?"

Deep breath. You can do this. She could tell this new friend of hers about the husband she had lost. She took a deep breath. "Alan loved God and country. And me and Sadie. He didn't plan on being career military. He wanted to be a doctor. He chose to be a medic instead. He even taught the other medics."

"Which explains why Sadie wanted to teach." Ben's tone was careful.

"Exactly." Vanessa wiped at a tear as it slid down her cheek. "Alan couldn't walk away. Not when the army needed him."

"He was a hero." Ben seemed to have almost a sense of brotherly care for Alan.

"Yes. Truly, he was." Vanessa let herself drift back. "Alan always made a point of being home at Christmas. When he could. When he wasn't deployed." She paused. This was the hardest part. "That early September morning . . . he was helping a wounded soldier outside Kandahar, just doing what he always did. Like you said, being a hero. When . . ."

Ben held on to every word.

"They hit an IED. Alan never saw it coming."

Ben seemed to be imagining the depth of loss Vanessa had faced. "It's not fair."

"No. But Sadie and I learned quickly that God wasn't the

reason for Alan's death. Even if He could've prevented it. God was our Rescue. Our Helper. We never could've survived without the Lord." She could see that more clearly now. "Even in the hardest times, we had God and each other."

Before Ben could respond, an actual trio of carolers entered the coffee shop. They were young and happy and loud, and once they were inside, they sang an a cappella version of "White Christmas." People in the café had no choice but to stop their conversations and listen.

Ben leaned closer to Vanessa. "All they need is a little gold paint."

Vanessa was still laughing when one of the carolers came up and took their hands. "Come on! Come sing with us!"

There was nothing Ben or Vanessa could do to dissuade the woman. So, with no warning or notice, Ben and Vanessa were suddenly part of the singing group. A quintet, apparently.

Ben caught Vanessa's gaze as they finished the song. "May your days be merry . . . and bright! And may all your Christmases be white!"

They were laughing so hard after that, they barely made it back to their table.

"I can't believe I did that." Ben took a long swig of his coffee. "Did that really happen?"

"Are you kidding me?" Vanessa dabbed at her eyes. This time because she was laughing too hard to catch her breath. "You were great."

"Me? You can really sing. You should join their group.

Hit the road." Ben wiped his eyes, too. "Maybe bring Maria and Leigh."

When the joy of the moment finally died down, Vanessa checked her phone. She had two text messages, both from Isaac Baker. Vanessa shared them with Ben. "Isaac texted."

"Isaac?" Ben raised his brow, teasing her. "Another friend?"

"Stop." She let out a single laugh. "Listen. He says he narrowed his search to a dozen stores. And they're all in Georgia!" Vanessa set her phone down and looked at Ben. "Do you think he might really be chasing after my ring?"

"It's possible." Ben looked around at the carolers and the café and finally at her. "The way this Christmas is going, I wouldn't be surprised."

And with that, Ben told her more than he had said all week. That maybe this wasn't just a friendship after all.

When they finished their coffee and were back outside, Ben turned to her. "Thank you for telling me about Alan." He put his hand on Vanessa's shoulder. "That meant a lot."

"You made it easy." Her heart felt light. Not at all the way she usually felt after talking about her husband.

"What?" He took a step closer to her.

"Letting you in." She touched his face with her hand the way she had once before. They started the walk back to her car and she thought of something. "You know what those one hundred little bears need?"

"One hundred families sponsored through Columbus Cares?" Ben shrugged. "Am I right?"

"Yes." She couldn't put into words how much she was

enjoying this. "But they need something else. Little collars that say, 'Take Me to College.'"

They reached her SUV and Ben took both her hands this time. "It'll be okay. Go home and talk to her. And tell her about me." He paused, his eyes and tone still light. "It's important."

"It is." Vanessa nodded. "She should be home in an hour."

"Okay, then." He pulled her into his arms, but again the hug didn't last long. "I'll see you tomorrow? Maybe we can actually shop for Christmas this time. In Old Town."

"I'd love that."

Long after she drove off, Vanessa wondered if she was reading Ben right. They both had past hurts, devastating losses. And she knew little about his. But she also found him holding back. Like during the hug just now.

The situation made Vanessa wonder exactly what she was going to tell Sadie. The last thing she wanted was to tell Sadie she was just friends with Ben when maybe . . . just maybe they were becoming something more.

Chapter 10

LONG AFTER DARK, VANESSA was still floating from her afternoon with Ben, still replaying their conversations and laughing at the way they had been talking about her sad story one minute and singing Christmas songs to the Harvest coffeehouse the next. Like they were a couple of traveling performers.

Every time she caught a glimpse of herself in the living room mirror, she was smiling. Even with things not quite right with Sadie.

Vanessa wasn't sure exactly what to make of her feelings. She and Ben had only spent a handful of days together in person. Still, he was all she could think about. They were getting together again tomorrow, and she could hardly wait.

The leftover lasagna sat back in the fridge, and Vanessa was about to text Sadie when she heard the front door open.

"Sorry I'm late!" Sadie sounded as happy as Vanessa. She shut the door and rounded the corner to the kitchen. "Mom, I promise I'll be around more! Ella's mom wanted to have me over for dinner before the holidays. But now"—Sadie flung her arms open—"I'm all yours!"

For the first time since Sadie had been home, things felt normal. Vanessa hugged her and thought for a moment. She needed to talk to Sadie, but maybe it was better if they had a little fun first. "Should we make Grandma's sugar cookies?"

"Should we?" Sadie grinned. "We have to! It's tradition!" She kept her arm around Vanessa. "And then let's watch *White Christmas*. We can't miss that."

"We *won't* miss it." Vanessa's heart took flight. Everything was going to be all right with Sadie. She was suddenly sure of it.

They found the flour and vanilla, the sugar and baking soda and salt, and Sadie pulled a pound of butter from the fridge. "Let's make lots." She looked at Vanessa. "Then we can take some to Hudson's mom."

"I love it. Maria and Leigh, too." Vanessa found a large mixing bowl and set it on the counter. "Leigh will be expecting a plate. You know she will."

They both laughed, rolled up their sleeves, and got to work. Vanessa played a list of Christmas oldies. She and Sadie sang along.

When the dough was mixed, they separated it into four balls. "That way the flour and butter stay blended." Sadie raised her brow. "I never forget these things, Mom. You taught me well."

They worked with one of the dough balls, using a rolling pin and parchment paper to make it the perfect thickness.

"You pick out the shapes." Vanessa nodded to the baking cupboard. "They're on the top shelf."

Sadie brought the bag down and opened it. "Let's both pick." She pulled a Christmas tree and star from the mix.

"I like that idea." Vanessa dusted her hands off and chose a Santa and a reindeer.

"Hey." It was Sadie's turn. "How about this heart?"

Again, Vanessa felt like she'd been caught. "The heart?"

"Sure." Sadie smiled at her. "Because love is always a part of Christmas."

"Love is. True." *Don't overreact.* "Jesus was the greatest gift of love."

"Exactly." Sadie set the heart with the other cookie cutters. "Love has always been at the middle of our Christmases, Mom. Hudson and I were talking about that earlier." She arranged the shapes. "I FaceTimed him at Ella's house."

"How is he?" Vanessa was happy to move the talk to Hudson. She certainly couldn't talk about Ben in the midst of a conversation about love.

Sadie's smile faded. "I don't know where they are, but he was down, Mom. Our call ended with sirens going off." She took the heart shape and pressed it into the dough. "That's happened before, but it just seems worse. I don't know."

Vanessa studied her daughter, the fear gathered at the corners of her eyes. "Let's pray for him. Right now."

For a moment Sadie looked like a little girl again. She reached out her hands, and Vanessa took hold of them. "I'd love that."

Her prayer was short and to the point. Vanessa asked God to send His guardian angels to surround Hudson wherever he was tonight, whatever mission he was working on. "Hudson is a soldier, and soldiers are always in danger, Lord." Vanessa paused. "But we trust You with Hudson. Be with him. That's all we ask of You. In Jesus' name, amen."

They were quiet, making cookie shapes and setting them on the baking sheet. Vanessa wondered if her thoughts were the same as Sadie's. Praying for the soldiers they loved did not guarantee them safe travels or perfect protection from danger. But talking to God about Hudson did assure them of the one thing that mattered most.

God would be with Sadie's young soldier as He had been with Alan.

Right up until his final breath.

They made four dozen cookies, many of them hearts, and frosted them with a homemade icing and every kind of red-and-green sprinkles. When the kitchen seemed covered in Christmas cookies, they changed into cozy pajamas and curled up under a blanket in the living room.

White Christmas was one of their favorite movies no matter what time of year. And of course it was, since it involved soldiers and the burden of far-off battles. They sipped hot chocolate and Sadie laid her head on Vanessa's shoulder as the movie came to an end.

This was all Vanessa had wanted since her daughter walked through the door a few nights ago. That the two of them would find again the connection they'd shared since Sadie was born. The one that had been especially close since

Alan died. *"You're all I have, Mom,"* Sadie had told her in the months after they laid Alan to rest. *"You're my best friend."*

When the credits finished, Vanessa flipped the screen to a cozy Christmas village with instrumental holiday tunes. She turned the volume down and shifted so she was looking at Sadie. "The ending gets better every time."

"It does." Sadie blinked back tears. "When he sees all his old soldiers gathered around to thank him, all I can see is Daddy. I wish that could have been his story. Living long enough to be celebrated by all the men he helped through the years."

"Sort of like when we watched *Scrooge*." Vanessa ran her hand over Sadie's hair. "You said Daddy knows the difference he made helping people through the years."

"Yes." Sadie seemed to think about that. "In heaven right now there are so many soldiers Dad helped. Men who didn't make it . . . just like him."

"I miss him." Vanessa meant it. Never mind how she was falling for Ben Miller. She would always miss Alan.

"I miss him, too." Sadie looked at the Christmas tree, at the photo ornaments that marked the branches.

"You know . . ." Vanessa smiled. "Your dad would do it all over again if he had to . . . That was him. Wired to help the hurting. Not just that, but to pray with them." Vanessa hadn't thought about this for a long time. "After a long deployment, your dad would come home and tell me about the guys he'd treated who weren't going to make it. He didn't just give them first aid, Sadie girl. He would tell them about Jesus." Vanessa paused. "He would ask them to cry out to the Lord for the only healing that lasts. The one that leads to salvation. And the men would do that."

The two of them reveled in that picture for a long moment. The man they loved, leading mortally wounded soldiers to the heart of God in their final minutes. Picturing that filled them with a joy that overpowered their sadness.

After the moment passed, Sadie talked about her classes and how at Reinhardt she'd taken photos of sporting events and concerts. "I have a gift for it, Mama. I really do."

"Of course you do." Vanessa smiled at her. "Can you show me?"

And Sadie did. She pulled up one photo after another, and she was right. "You're so talented, honey. We wouldn't want a girl who can take photos like this wasting away in the wrong classes, now would we?"

They both laughed, an easy sort of laugh that assured Vanessa again that everything was going to be okay between them. Which meant . . . maybe this was the time to bring up Ben. "I've been trying to talk to you about something since you got home. But we've both been busy."

Sadie straightened and looked at her, curious. "I'm here now." Her voice was kind. "Tell me."

"Right. Well . . ." There was no turning back. "I was wondering, honey. What would you think if I started . . . you know, seeing someone?"

"Seeing someone?" Her daughter looked baffled. "Like a therapist?"

Maybe this was a bad idea. Vanessa shook her head. "No.

Not like that." She paused. "I mean, what would you think if I started dating?"

The words felt like sandpaper on Vanessa's tongue. She regretted them immediately.

"What?" Sadie stared at her and then pushed the blanket off her lap. She stood, her face frozen. A frustrated laugh came from her. "You and I have the best night and then . . . I sure wasn't expecting this."

Vanessa wanted a do-over. Anything to take her words back. "I just thought if we—"

"What about Dad? Have you thought about him?" Sadie paced to the tree, putting more space between them.

Shock came over Vanessa. She stood and walked to Sadie. "Of course I've thought about him. I wanted to live my whole life with your father. But at a certain point . . ." She put her hand on Sadie's shoulder.

But her daughter pulled away.

"Sadie."

"No." She studied Vanessa's face. "Are you asking? Or are you already seeing someone?"

"Well, that's what—"

"I can't do this." Sadie stepped back. "Look, Mom, do what you want. I don't want to talk about it. Not now." She held up one hand and turned to leave.

"Sadie, I thought we could just talk about it." Vanessa moved to follow her but then stopped.

Sadie looked over her shoulder as she walked away. "I can't do this tonight. I'm tired."

"Honey, I'm sorry . . . I didn't want . . ."

"It's okay. I'm fine. Just tired." And with that, Sadie left the room.

Vanessa felt fresh tears well in her eyes. After the beautiful night they'd shared, Sadie's reaction told Vanessa one thing. The reason she hadn't brought up Ben before was because her feelings for him had never been only friendship related.

In slow motion Vanessa dropped to the floor and sat cross-legged in front of the tree. How could she move on with Ben if Sadie felt like this? But then, why had God brought Ben into her life in the first place?

Sadie would come around, right? Or maybe she wouldn't.

Vanessa's heart hung in a ball of knots, and she realized there was just one way to handle her fear. The same way she had helped Sadie earlier. She would pray. For the next hour Vanessa did just that.

She prayed for a miracle.

That somehow she could have the love of both Sadie and the man she couldn't stop thinking about. *Please, God.* She closed her eyes. *Please make a way.* She wouldn't move ahead without Sadie's approval.

But already she couldn't imagine a life without Ben Miller.

By the next morning Vanessa had more peace about the situation with Sadie. Her daughter was bound to react that way the first time Vanessa brought up the idea of dating. But she would come around. And in time—if Vanessa and Ben did start dating—Sadie would understand.

Vanessa was sure of it. One way or another, they would

have to finish their conversation before the dance. Because Ben was going as her date. That much was already decided.

Even if it was the only date they ever had.

THE SITUATION with Sadie was beginning to worry Ben. He and Vanessa were walking down Broadway in Old Town. The sky was blue, the air was cool, and Christmas filled every window and corner.

If only Vanessa's heart didn't seem so heavy.

"What did you tell her?" Ben glanced her way. Their pace was easy, the whole day ahead of them. Ben kept his tone even. "I mean, when you brought up the idea of me?"

Vanessa uttered a sad laugh. "I didn't get that far."

"Because . . ." Ben stopped and faced her. "You brought up the idea of having a guy friend, and she ran out of the room."

"Not exactly." She hesitated. "It's all sort of a blur."

Ben nodded. "Okay." He kept walking. "You'll figure it out."

"I will." She seemed relieved at the thought. Just then her phone buzzed. "Hold on." She stopped and pulled it from her purse. "It's Isaac."

"Isaac who might have found your ring?" Ben had wondered if the guy was making progress.

"Wait!" Vanessa stopped again. She read the text once more and then held both hands straight in the air. "He found it! Ben, he found it! He has it narrowed down to six stores now, and he's sure my ring is at one of them."

Unless the buyer had already sold it. Ben didn't mention the possibility. Best to let Vanessa think she was onto something. He liked seeing her smile.

"I think this might actually be real." She put her phone back in her purse. "Can you imagine, after all this time? This guy might be the answer to years of prayers!" She raised her brow. "It's Sadie's ring, too. I was going to give it to her on her college graduation, the way my mom gave it to me for mine."

Vanessa's enthusiasm was contagious. "Well, there you go!" Ben picked her up and swung her around. The sound of her laughter was everything. When he set her down, Ben kept his arms around her waist. "Looks like it could be a happy Christmas after all."

"It does look that way, doesn't it?" If Vanessa's eyes were any indication, she was falling for him as deeply as he had long ago fallen for her.

For the first time, Ben took her hand in his, and the connection was electric. That's how they walked down the street, and Ben made a promise to himself. He would pray for Sadie and he would believe God would work things out. Because now that Vanessa's hand was in his, Ben was convinced of one very beautiful truth.

He didn't ever want to let go.

THE SHOPPING trip with Ella and Cami was just what Sadie needed. Why had her mom ruined such a great night by bringing up dating? Now, of all times, in the middle of Christmas? Maybe her mother's loneliness had gotten to be too much lately. Or maybe she was lonely because Sadie had been busy with Hudson and Ella. Her mother was probably imagining her life all alone, and she might have figured it was a good time to talk with Sadie about the possibility of dating.

Whatever the situation, her mother was wrong. The timing was totally off. Sadie hadn't given the idea any thought since then. This morning before she left the house, she'd asked her mom to come shopping with her and the girls. They had planned on going to the mall, and at first it seemed like her mom wanted to join them. But she told Sadie she was working on the dance. She had donations to pick up and decorations to buy.

"Maybe another time." Sadie had kissed her cheek before leaving. "I'm not mad. I just . . . don't want to talk about you . . . you know." Sadie hadn't been able to finish her sentence. "You get it, right?"

"I do." Her mom had not pushed the issue. Sadie was more than glad.

Now she and Ella and Cami had ditched the idea of the mall. They were on Broadway in Old Town, shopping for their families and boyfriends. Sadie had already decided to get Hudson a new wallet and her mom a sweater. The winter cold seemed determined to stay, so that would be perfect.

They were at Sandra's Boutique where the clothes were the cutest when Cami gave Sadie a light shove. "Hey, is that your mom?"

"What?" Sadie had a sweater in her hands. She couldn't tell if it was too bright for her mother.

"Your mom." Cami shoved her again. "Look! With that guy!"

Sadie dropped the sweater and joined Cami and Ella at the store window. She got there just in time to see the last glimpse of a couple walking down the street. The woman wore a ponytail and the guy was tall. No one Sadie had ever seen. "That's not her."

"Definitely not." Ella put her hands on her hips and stared at Cami. "Are you out of your mind? Sadie's mom with some guy?"

The moment passed and Sadie picked up the sweater from the floor. She dusted it off and changed her mind. Way too bright. But the whole time one question pressed against her mind.

Had her mom been wearing a ponytail that morning? No. Right? She dismissed the thought. There were a dozen reasons why that woman couldn't have been her mother. First of all, her mom wasn't dating. She definitely would have told Sadie if she was. She took a deep breath and let the idea go. It was nothing more than the obvious.

Cami's overactive imagination.

THE RING needed a better container, so Howard found one in the back room. A deep green velvet box with old hinges and a soft white satin pillow. The rightful spot for the heirloom to rest on. No matter how often he thought about the ring, he still couldn't believe it was worth twenty-five thousand dollars.

Today's stream of customers at Millers' Antiques had been impressive, even for five days before Christmas. He and Gary hadn't had five minutes for their chess game, and even now they had a line at both registers.

"There you go." Howard handed a man two bags. "Excellent choices, sir. Have a merry Christmas."

"You," Gary uttered under his breath. "You've been smiling since you got in."

"Take a look at that ring, Gary. It's locked up under the counter." He kept his voice to a low whisper. "You'd be smiling, too."

A woman approached them. "I'm looking for an old Bible. I heard you have a section."

"That we do!" The line was down now, so Howard walked off with the woman. "There's something very special about holding an old Bible, knowing that someone long ago found life and comfort in the words. And now someone new can find that same help today." Howard looked over his shoulder at Gary. "Check out the ring!"

"You've lost it, Howard."

Howard chuckled. He enjoyed the friendship he and Gary shared, the way they both loved antiques and the customers who came through the doors.

After Howard took the woman to the old Bible section, he returned to the register. Finally the steady traffic had eased enough for Gary to get the ring from the cabinet. He held it up. "It's a beaut." He shook his head. "I never would've guessed it was real."

"But it is. You're holding twenty-five thousand dollars, cousin."

Gary squinted at the inside of the ring. "Well, look at that. It's engraved."

"It's not." Howard leaned against the counter. "The thing is more than a hundred years old. That's what the jeweler said. But it's not engraved. Those are scratches."

"Did you ask if it was engraved?" Gary looked up. He blinked a few times.

"Of course not." He didn't hesitate. "Why would I ask that? There's nothing on the inside of that band. It's scratched. That's it."

Gary studied it again. Two more customers entered the store. He shrugged and put the ring back in the box. "You might be right." He locked it in the cabinet beneath the counter.

The first customer headed for Howard. She had a little girl with her. "We're looking for an antique clock." She smiled at the little girl. "For her daddy."

"Ah, the gift of time." Howard stepped out from behind the counter. "Follow me." This time he looked back at Gary and called out, "I'm getting you new glasses for Christmas, Gary. You need 'em."

Howard turned his attention to the woman and little girl. "I think you'll find we have a tremendous array of old clocks and watches. Because the gift of time is the greatest gift of all."

Howard led them to the right section. But all he could think about was the obvious. In three days he'd have that twenty-five thousand dollars.

And he'd be one day closer to that trip to Italy.

Chapter 11

THEY WERE STILL HOLDING hands.

That was all Vanessa could think about as she and Ben walked into the oldest bookstore in Columbus. Ben still had hold of her hand. The touch of his fingers against hers, the way it felt to walk at his side with their hands connected... It was a feeling Vanessa never thought she'd feel again.

She had thought if they got to this point in their friendship, if things took a romantic turn, then she'd feel guilty about Alan. But she didn't. Instead, the way her heart and feet floated along beside Ben made her happier than she'd felt in years. Happy and beyond hopeful.

Vanessa knew the old bookstore well. She led Ben to the back and a section of vintage poetry books. Ben's eyes lit up as they reached the shelves. He reached for one by Walt Whitman. "Are you kidding me?"

"I saved the best for last." Vanessa stood a few feet from him, studying him. Thrilled by him. "I figured they'd still have the Whitman book."

Ben thumbed through it. "Most people don't think Walt was a believer."

"I've read that." Vanessa angled her head, imagining the brilliant mind of Whitman and his complicated beliefs. "He's credited with being a skeptic. The founder of a new religion that sort of broke the bonds of traditional beliefs."

Ben glanced at Vanessa. "I don't agree with all that. Walt believed God was in all created things. That always made sense to me." He lowered the book and looked out the nearby window. "For me, I see God in the sky and stars, the flowers and fields. I see Him there because those are His creations."

"Mmm." Vanessa followed his gaze. "When Sadie was little, she would create these pretty paintings and we'd hang them on the fridge." She smiled, lost in the memory. "When she'd be at school, I would walk by and see her creation. And I'd see her, too. Because she made that drawing. Everything about those art pieces had her written into the design."

"I knew you'd get it." Ben held up the book. "This one is for you." He set it aside and turned his attention back to the shelves of antique books. "We always wanted a section like this in the store. There just isn't room."

Vanessa thumbed through a few of the titles. "My mom used to say if we lose the old books, we lose history itself."

"And when do I get to meet *her*?" He chuckled.

"Maybe the morning after the dance." She smiled. "My parents live in Florida. They work full time for a church there. No retiring for those two." She laughed. "But they're coming for a few weeks on Christmas Eve."

"Your mom sounds very wise."

"They both are. I got my love for the poets and old writers from them." Vanessa turned to him. "And you?"

"My love for poetry came from my dad. How he loves old things. But it was my wife who taught me the love of books." He paused. "On our first anniversary she bought me a set of US history titles. No agenda back then. Just history."

"Tell me about her." Vanessa's voice was soft. "Will you?"

From the beginning with Vanessa, Ben hadn't talked about Laura. Not any more than Vanessa had talked about Alan. But here, lost in the shelves of ancient words and fragile tomes, he seemed to let the past come to life. If only for a few moments.

"Laura was my high school sweetheart. She was there for our shop's grand opening." His smile softened. "She always thought our kids would run the place someday."

Vanessa let that settle. "What happened?"

"She had health issues from the beginning. We found out she couldn't have children, then a few days before her thirty-fourth birthday, she got her diagnosis." He sighed. "She was gone ten months later."

"That's a lot."

"I told you about my men's Bible study. The guy who leads it helped me navigate that time. I never lost hope, but it took time."

"So . . . eight years ago."

"Eight summers. Summer was our season." He reached out and touched Vanessa's arm. "I never thought there'd be anyone else. I couldn't imagine finding . . . you."

"Me either." Vanessa covered his hand with her own and their eyes held. "I never dreamed I'd be—"

"Excuse me." A fancy woman in her late sixties stepped by them. "I need to see this shelf."

Vanessa and Ben stepped in opposite directions to make room for her. Ben's eyes met Vanessa's and the two covered a laugh. So much for privacy. The woman sorted through a quick handful of books and grabbed an old copy of a Ray Bradbury classic. She held it up with the hint of a smile. "Carry on."

Vanessa felt like a schoolgirl caught talking in the library. "She must be fun at the holidays."

"Eccentric is always fun." Ben chuckled.

Vanessa surveyed the store. No one else seemed to desperately need a vintage book from this section. For now, they were alone again. She couldn't look away from Ben. She felt completely taken by him. "Where were we?"

Ben kept his distance, but he reached for her hand once more. "Right about here, I believe."

"Yes. That was it." She searched his eyes. Suddenly she no longer worried about being too honest with him. "You're leaving in an hour. Why is that all I can think about?"

"Just for the night." He never looked away. "I'll take the treasures home to my dad and be back tomorrow afternoon." He stepped toward her, almost closing the gap between them. "And tomorrow night . . ." He ran his thumb over her hand. "Tomorrow, could I take you out on a date?"

She could feel her cheeks blush. Something that happened often when she was with him. "I'd like that very much."

"Okay then." He smiled. "It's settled."

He bought the Walt Whitman and another one—an American classic poetry collection—for his shop back in Marietta. "It'll be nice seeing it on the shelves," he told her as they waited at the register. "As long as it lasts, anyway."

Vanessa pulled her sweater closer. The bookstore was drafty and today was chillier than yesterday. "How come that one?"

"Because." His eyes sparkled. "It reminds me of you. An American classic."

Again, he looked like he wanted to take her in his arms, but Vanessa knew he wouldn't. This was her hometown and people might catch on to the fact that Vanessa Mayfield wasn't chumming around with merely a good friend. Anyone could see they were already so much more.

The store owner approached and rang up the sale.

"Mr. Wright." Vanessa nodded at him. She cast a glance at Ben. Her look told him she knew the man. Vanessa looked at the owner again. "Are you ready for Christmas?"

"I am. My wife's already cooking." The man looked at Ben and then Vanessa. Clearly, he knew something was up. He winked at Vanessa. "Seems you found what you were looking for."

Vanessa's smile felt as genuine as the Georgia sun. She cast Ben another quick look and then she smiled at the shop owner again. "Yes, sir. I believe I have."

Once they were out front, Ben handed her the Walt Whitman book. "To the only other person I know who can quote Mr. Whitman."

Vanessa was touched to the depths of her soul. She took the gift and studied it. "Thank you."

This time, Ben didn't seem to care if the shop owner was watching. He drew Vanessa into his arms. She held on to him as tightly as he held on to her. Until the chill in the air disappeared and all she could feel was the warmth of his body against hers.

If only he would kiss her and tell her how he really felt, how he couldn't imagine being only her friend. *In time. Give it time.*

"I like this." He leaned back enough to see her face. "I don't want to let you go."

"Same." She put her hand alongside his face. "This doesn't feel real."

"But it is."

She could feel Ben's breath near her hair. A joy welled up inside her.

"Walk me to my truck?"

Vanessa nodded and he took her hand again. This time he slid his fingers between hers and they walked more slowly than before. Because Vanessa could tell she wasn't the only one. Neither of them wanted to say goodbye. Not for one day.

Not now. Not ever.

ALL BEN wanted was to kiss her goodbye.

But he wouldn't dare think about it. Not unless he knew

for sure that she was ready. His plan was straightforward. He would take her to dinner tomorrow night and ask her to be his girlfriend. If she was okay with the timing, then after that there would be no more wondering.

And a year from now, who knew?

They reached his truck at the quiet end of the street, and he slid his bags into the back seat with the others. Then he turned to her. "I'll pick you up at your house tomorrow. Five o'clock okay?"

A slight hesitation crossed her face. "Text me. In case I haven't had time to talk to Sadie."

"She's shopping?"

"Yes. At the mall with her friends. She asked me to go." Vanessa lifted one shoulder. "We keep missing each other."

"Maybe tonight, then." He didn't want to push. But there had to be some way to get past this part. "It's still true. I can't wait to meet her."

"You're patient, Ben." Vanessa took his hand this time. "Thank you."

He had to get on the road, but not before holding her once more. He eased his arms around her waist, and she slipped hers around his neck. Like a couple of teenagers slow-dancing in the gym, they stayed that way.

"I can't wait for tomorrow." He let himself get lost in her eyes. "Our first date."

"I was wondering if you'd ask me." Her eyes shone. "You know, since we were only friends."

Like gravity, he felt himself being pulled to her. But just when they might've shared their first kiss, a sidewalk Santa walked by, ringing the loudest bell Ben had ever heard.

Over the sound he motioned his thumb at the guy. "I know that bell." Ben had to practically yell over the sound. "Eighteen twelve."

"That right?" Vanessa raised her voice, too. They both laughed.

"Merry Christmas, folks!" The Santa waved at them. "Merry Christmas!"

The moment broken, Ben stepped back. He kissed Vanessa's forehead and climbed into his truck. "I'll text you when I get back to town."

"Okay. I'll talk to Sadie tonight."

In response Ben only smiled. He started his truck, waved once more, and drove away. The minute he hit the highway, he did something he'd been doing a lot of lately.

Counting the minutes until he could see Vanessa again.

SADIE WATCHED the man's truck drive away, and then she saw her mom get into her car and head the other direction. Sadie dropped to the sill of the store's front window and covered her face with her hands.

What had she just witnessed? She tried to draw a full breath, but she couldn't. Her heart was in her throat and her lungs felt too tight. The images played in her mind again and made her dizzy.

She had been looking at a purse near the front window when the same couple walked by, the one Cami had seen earlier. Only this time Cami and Ella were trying on jeans at the back of the store.

The windows must've been tinted because the couple didn't see Sadie. Good thing. As soon as they came into view, Sadie gasped. "What in the world . . . ?" Her words had been a whisper, an attempt to catch her breath. Sadie had frozen in place. She could do nothing but watch because Cami had been right.

Chestnut ponytail bouncing behind her, the woman walking hand in hand with some guy was indeed her mother. And the man . . . Sadie had no idea who he was. But they were holding hands like they were the only two people in the world. Sadie hadn't ever seen her mom look so happy—or at least not in four years.

They reached his truck and they hugged. For a long time. It looked like they might kiss, but one of those bell-ringing Santas seemed to interrupt the moment. And then the guy got in his truck and drove off.

So what was this? Sadie leaned on the window frame so she wouldn't pass out. Her mom was dating someone? All this time? Without telling her?

In a rush Sadie remembered her mom's question the other day. *What if she wanted to see someone? Could it maybe be time?* And Sadie had refused to talk about it.

That wasn't her mother's fault—it was hers.

Sadie stood and gathered herself. She pushed her feelings aside. Her friends would wonder what was wrong if Sadie didn't act normal, and she wasn't about to tell them what she'd just witnessed. Not until she talked things out with her mom.

Which was what she should have done the other night,

no matter how shocked or hurt Sadie was by the idea. Because clearly it wasn't a matter of whether it was *time* for her mom to date again.

Rather, the question was, *who* was she dating?

And how could she so quickly forget about Dad?

Chapter 12

SOMETHING WAS OFF WITH Sadie, Vanessa could tell that much. She just had no idea what it was. Hudson, maybe. The danger he'd been in lately. Whatever her problem, they'd have to talk about it later.

The Columbus Cares Annual Christmas Military Dance was in two days, and this morning was the first time they were allowed into the Veterans' Hall to bring the place to life. Sadie seemed happier once they started working. They brought ten bags in from the car and then stood in the entrance watching dozens of volunteers scramble in different directions.

"Okay, Mom." Sadie looped her arm through Vanessa's, the way she'd done when she was younger. "What should we do first?"

Vanessa checked her list. Maria was overseeing the assembling and decorating of the Christmas trees, and Leigh was helping a team of college kids set up thirty round tables that would frame the dance floor. In the next two days the other women on the committee would bring tablecloths, centerpieces, and garland.

The hall was about to be transformed into a Christmas wonderland.

Along one wall a series of tables had been set up for the team working to assemble the baskets for the sponsored families. "Let's start there." Vanessa walked toward the tables and Sadie followed.

Vanessa glanced at her daughter. "Thanks for helping."

"Of course." Sadie pushed up the sleeves of her sweater. "I look forward to this every year."

It was true. The dance was something they always pulled off together.

The first annual military dance had taken place right after they had returned from Breckenridge, that vacation they took months after Alan had been killed. The one when she had lost her Christmas ring.

They made that first dance in late December so they could always take the Colorado Christmas trip earlier in the month. And even though they hadn't gone back to Breckenridge since Sadie was a high school sophomore, prepping for the dance was fun for them both.

"Getting the baskets ready will take all day," Vanessa said. "So many donated items this year."

They unpacked one bag after another, setting out the largest items first. Old Town Market had donated a ten-pound bag of organic flour for each family. Vanessa and Sadie started there.

They lined up ten empty baskets. Then one at a time they put a flour bag at the center. "This is going to work." Sadie laughed. "Nothing else we give them could possibly be bigger than that."

There were other food items and books that framed out the back side of the baskets. They were about to open the bag of teddy bears when Leigh and Maria came running from across the hall.

"Mrs. Benson needs us." Leigh waved her arms. "Something terrible happened!"

Vanessa and Sadie left the baskets and met Leigh and Maria. Vanessa faced her friend. "Slower, Leigh. What is it?"

"The wind! Mrs. Benson was hanging garland, and that wind we've had lately was just too much. Too windy." Leigh took a quick breath.

They were getting nowhere. Maria held up her hand. "Let me tell it." She turned to Vanessa and Sadie. "Mrs. Benson fell off her ladder. She went to the hospital last night and turns out she broke her ankle. The high school group is already at the house, but they need a few adults to supervise."

"Oh no. Poor Mrs. Benson." Sadie grabbed her purse. "We can help. Come on, Mom, let's go."

Vanessa found her bag and made a plan with her two friends. "Sadie and I will take care of Mrs. Benson. You two stay and oversee the decorating. We'll be back as soon as we can."

"This is what Columbus Cares is all about." Maria smiled at Vanessa and Sadie. "Go make a difference."

On the ride to Mrs. Benson's, Vanessa looked at her daughter. "I'm proud of you. For stepping up like this."

"Thanks." Sadie gave Vanessa's hand a sweet squeeze. "I learned it from you. Plus, Mrs. Benson is military. She's one of us. Part of the family."

In the background Michael Bublé's "I'll Be Home for Christmas" played from Vanessa's phone. She waited a moment. "You seemed a little quiet this morning. Everything okay with Hudson?"

"It is." Sadie looked more relaxed. "We talked last night. He didn't seem as down."

"That's good. I ask God every day to protect him."

For a minute it seemed Sadie might say more, as if there really was something on her mind, but just then they pulled up to Mrs. Benson's house and the moment passed.

"Oh dear." Vanessa cut the engine and stared out at the woman's front yard. Kids were moving trash cans and boxes of decorations and bush clippings in what felt like barely organized chaos. Others hung lights in the tree out front. And there was Mrs. Benson, sitting in one of her high-backed velvet dining room chairs in the middle of the yard.

Giving out orders.

"Yep." Sadie allowed a quiet laugh. "That's Mrs. Benson."

"Let's do this." Vanessa led the way as she and Sadie walked up to the older woman. Mrs. Benson's ankle might have been broken, but nothing was wrong with her voice.

"You over there." The woman cupped her hands around her mouth so the students hanging garland on her porch could hear her. "A little higher, please. That's right. No, a little higher still. More."

There wasn't a stitch of meanness or lack of gratitude in Mrs. Benson. But she had a particular way about her. And if the kids were going to help her, she was going to tell them how to do it.

Vanessa reached her first. "Mrs. Benson." She put her hand on the woman's shoulder. "Should you be out here? Your foot's in a cast. Maybe it should be elevated."

"No, dear." Mrs. Benson looked past Vanessa. "Sadie Mayfield, aren't you the spitting image of your beautiful mama. I see college is agreeing with you."

"Yes, ma'am." Sadie sidled up next to Vanessa. "Can we help you back to the house?"

"Not at all." The woman cupped her hands around her mouth again and yelled at two other teens, "See that branch that hangs down? Make sure it has less lights than the others. That way no one will see the thing's about to fall off the tree. That's right. A little less."

A teenager feebly shouted back, "Yes, ma'am. Thank you."

Mrs. Benson turned to Vanessa again. "You know what they gave me at the hospital? A scooter." She looked at Sadie. "Can you believe that? A scooter! As if this old woman is going to bebop around the neighborhood on a scooter!"

"Actually..." Vanessa folded her arms. What was she going to do with the woman? "I think it's more about keeping weight off your broken ankle."

"Fine, but a scooter?" She looked at Sadie again. "You still dating that handsome army Ranger of yours, missy?"

"I am. He can't make it home for Christmas." Sadie looked disappointed. "Of course, that's part of the job."

"It is, my dear. That it is."

Vanessa took note. Maybe that was the problem. The closer they got to Christmas, the more Sadie missed Hudson.

Mrs. Benson yelled again. "The garland has to go closer to the roofline. Yes! That's it."

"So what happened?" Vanessa studied the woman's cast. It went nearly to her knee.

"Oh, that wind." The woman waved her hand like she was shooing away a fly. "I do believe it's the windiest December in ages." She pointed to the ladder, the one the teenage boys were using. "I was up on the ladder hanging my lights just fine all by myself when a gust came up and blew me right to the ground."

"I suppose it goes without saying, Mrs. Benson"—Vanessa smiled—"that at your age you probably shouldn't be climbing ladders."

"Now Vanessa, I'm fine on a ladder. Just not on a windy day." She motioned to the house. "And now I have six high schoolers cleaning my living room and not one of them knows where to find the Windex."

Vanessa nodded. "Okay. You stay here. Sadie and I will take the house."

Half an hour later things on the inside were under control. Sadie worked on the laundry. Already the towels were folded, and two more loads were being washed and dried. At the same time, the students had vacuumed the house and tidied the main rooms.

Mrs. Benson needed more help than Vanessa had realized. She worked in the kitchen, cleaning the woman's stove. Sadie came up to her and leaned against the kitchen counter. "You're amazing, Mom." She watched Vanessa. "This whole Columbus Cares thing is because of you."

"And your dad." Vanessa felt a wave of sorrow. The way she didn't often feel it anymore. "This is just what he always wanted. A way for the military families to help their own."

"Well . . . he'd be proud of you." Sadie looked around. "You made it happen."

"We all did. You, me, Leigh, Maria. So many people." Vanessa never felt like it was her idea alone. There were more than a hundred thousand military family members in Columbus after all. Many people did what they could to help, even beyond the year-round assistance from Columbus Cares.

Sadie was quiet for a beat. "Can I tell you something? I'm sorry for cutting you off the other night. When you wanted to talk."

The admission surprised Vanessa. She slipped her arm around Sadie's shoulders. "Don't worry about it, honey. We can talk later. It wasn't the best timing on my part."

They both laughed. Ten minutes later when things were sufficiently under control, she and Sadie helped Mrs. Benson back to her house. The woman used the scooter to get set up in her recliner. "The pillows on that far sofa should be straighter." Mrs. Benson smiled. "If y'all wouldn't mind."

Vanessa and Sadie laughed again. The sensation felt wonderful, she and Sadie sharing the humor of their time at Mrs. Benson's house.

And later, Vanessa would find time to bring up the idea of dating and the specifics about Ben. Sadie looked ready to talk, and that was all Vanessa could ask for.

✶

THE BACK room at Millers' Antiques was overrun with boxes when Ben set to work that day. He wasn't going to return to Columbus until tomorrow morning. He'd already told Vanessa. Too much work to do here to help his dad.

Before working on the cardboard boxes that had arrived while he was gone, Ben went through the bags of things he'd bought in Columbus. He would remove the item from its bag, take off the tag, and polish it up. Then his dad would bounce into the back room and scurry the items out to the storefront.

Just four days till Christmas and things were flying off the shelves.

His dad returned from the shop. "It's hopping out there."

"God has blessed us, that's for sure." Ben pulled an old typewriter from a box of heavier Columbus items. "Look at this relic."

His father marveled at the piece. "Gotta be two hundred years old."

"That's just about right." Ben chuckled. "You know your antiques."

"Speaking of which." His dad pierced the air with his pointer finger. "I haven't shown you my treasure."

"No." Ben smiled at him. "No, you haven't."

"I'll be right back." With great care his father carried the typewriter toward the storefront. "I'm putting this right up in the window."

"It'll be gone before Christmas." Ben pulled the fountain pen from a bag.

"Are you kidding? It'll be gone by tomorrow."

Something caught Ben's eye. A bookcase that usually stood in the center of the store was broken. Must've happened while he was in Columbus. Ben would fix it before he left town again.

In no time his dad returned. He held a small green velvet box and handed it to Ben. "When was the last time you held a twenty-five-thousand-dollar piece of jewelry?"

"Uh, never." Ben grinned as he took the box.

From the front of the store, they heard Gary yell, "Howard, get back here! Someone has a question about the typewriter."

His father shook his head and hurried for the front. "Why do I even have a clerk?"

Ben chuckled. The two men were quite the pair.

He opened the small velvet box, and what he saw caught his heart. The ring had a ruby center and a ring of diamonds. He had never seen an actual picture of Vanessa's missing ring, but this had to look a lot like it.

There was one difference, of course. Vanessa's was a costume piece. This one was real. Ben took the ring from the box and studied the stone, the diamonds. He'd seen one like it on eBay not long ago. He had been looking for Vanessa's ring. One ruby diamond ring was listed at over a million dollars. Another for nearly a hundred thousand.

He had a feeling the buyer was getting a steal purchasing this one for a fourth of that. But that's what the appraiser had said it was worth, and people who valued jewelry were almost never wrong.

At least in Ben's experience with antiques.

There were markings on the inside of the band. Ben looked closely and saw a word nearly worn off. It was in cursive and appeared to be French. *Maison.* He whispered the word. He studied it again. "Interesting." He slipped the ring back into the box and set the box down on the bench beside him.

Then he began singing. It was his favorite way to pass the time when he was logging in antiques for the store. He thought about the time he and Vanessa sang at the Harvest coffeehouse when he'd first landed in Columbus. The memory made him laugh. He was about to sing the same song from that day. But at the last minute he changed his mind and sang the only words that fit the way he was about to spend the rest of the week.

"I'll be home for Christmas . . . You can count on me . . ." He sang the song and worked through the antiques and dreamed of just one thing.

His trip back to Columbus.

VANESSA AND Sadie were back at the Veterans' Hall working on the baskets again. They had nearly finished the first ten and were about to put the teddy bears in.

Sadie picked up one of them. "Hey, it's like my bear at home."

"Yes." Vanessa smiled at her. "Karl from Karl's Toys donated a hundred of them." She looked at the bear. "Every one of them reminds me of you."

"Mmm. Mom." Sadie picked up a bear and situated it in one of the baskets. "That's so sweet."

"Like you." Vanessa checked her list. "Sixty families are sponsored so far. The radio's pushing for more people to step up. That's going on all day. We'll get there. I believe that."

"I didn't tell you. I want to sponsor a family." Sadie placed another bear in a different basket. "Hudson wants to take one, too. He told me to tell you."

"Honey." Vanessa shook her head. "You need to save your money for books and clothes. You're in school."

"Mom, I want to do this." Sadie seemed certain. "It's my Christmas present to myself. And I have savings."

"Okay." Vanessa let it go. She smiled at her daughter. "You have your father's heart."

"And your hands." Sadie relaxed. "I really want to do this."

"Well, then. We only need thirty-eight more sponsors."

Vanessa's phone rang. She stepped away and pulled it from her purse. "Hello?"

"Mrs. Mayfield? This is Isaac Baker."

"Yes." Vanessa returned to Sadie's side. She whispered to her daughter, "It's the guy looking for my ring." She put the call on speakerphone. "Is there an update, Isaac?"

"I've narrowed it down to three stores. All in northern Georgia. I'm sure one of them has your jewelry. I had it in my store and I sent it in a box to one of them. I should know more in the next forty-eight hours. I have calls in to all three shops."

Vanessa felt tears well in her eyes. "Are you serious?"

"Are you serious about the reward?" Isaac laughed. "I mean, I'm doing this for a reason, Mrs. Mayfield."

"I'm serious." Vanessa looked at Sadie. "That ring belongs to me, but it also belongs to my daughter. Please... let me know what you find."

The call ended and Vanessa pulled Sadie into a hug. "What if he really finds it?"

"What you just said." Sadie eased back and searched Vanessa's eyes. "You mean that? The ring is mine?"

"On your college graduation day. Yes." Vanessa kissed Sadie's cheek. "That's when my mom gave it to me."

"The whole thing seems too good to be true. Like every other time." Sadie sighed. "But I'm going to pray. Because if this is real, then you might have your ring back in time for Christmas."

The possibility was too great for Vanessa to imagine. While they continued placing bears in the baskets, she and Sadie talked about that long-ago Breckenridge trip. How they had tumbled down the hill at the end of the sledding run and how Vanessa hadn't had her gloves. Finding the ring now would be a miracle.

A thought occurred to Vanessa. This was the year God had brought more than one miracle into her life. So maybe it was possible, after all.

First Ben Miller. And now, just maybe, her long-lost Christmas ring.

Chapter 13

EVERY MILE FELT LONGER than the last as Ben made his way from Marietta back to Columbus. God had been so good to him, letting him meet Vanessa and build a friendship over the last half a year.

But now to think he was about to take her on a date? It was more than Ben could've hoped for. After losing Laura, he never thought he'd date again. Sure, he was still young, but he and Laura had gone through so much together. Who else would ever connect with him the way she had? Or build a life with him the way she had?

That all had changed at the Christmas-in-July sale. Since then, Ben's greatest concern was moving slowly enough not to scare Vanessa away. But those concerns eased the minute she said yes to this date. Which meant he could start treating her the way he'd been dying to treat her.

Like a woman he was interested in.

And not merely like a friend.

He stopped at the florist not far from Vanessa's house and picked up something special for her. Something he'd been longing to do since they met. Sadie was spending the night at Ella's house, so again he wouldn't be meeting Vanessa's daughter tonight.

Ben felt his heart thud against his chest as he made his way up her sidewalk. He wore a navy blazer and dark jeans. When she answered the door, she looked surprised. But not as surprised as he was.

"Look at you." He stayed on the front porch. "You're beautiful, Vanessa."

Her red silk jacket and white turtleneck made her look like someone in a magazine. Her delicate cheekbones and flawless skin took his breath. He wondered if she would ask him inside, but their dinner reservations were only an hour from then.

She stepped out and locked the door behind her. "I've never seen you dressed up."

"I couldn't. Not if we were just friends." He grinned at her. Then he pulled out the plastic box and removed the white wrist corsage inside. "These are old-fashioned, I know." He smiled. "I don't care." He slipped it over her fingers and set it in place. "Because every girl deserves a corsage."

They parked on the other side of Old Town Square and took their time walking to Emilio's. The Christmas tree at the center of Old Town rose high above the street, shining with thousands of lights and handmade ornaments from the children of Columbus.

"Have I mentioned I love this place?" Ben took in the sight of Vanessa. The night was chilly again, so he put his arm around her. A couple passing by took their picture by the tree, and then they stopped in at an antique store they'd somehow missed. At one of the front tables, a display of vintage frames caught Ben's attention.

"I might get a few of these." He picked up one of them. The frame was wrapped in a floral cloth, finely put together and yellowed with time. He flipped it over. "Nineteen forty-two." He smiled at her. "My turn."

"I can't wait." Vanessa was glowing.

Ben looked at the frame, then back at Vanessa. "She worked at the Red Cross and pined for her young GI."

"World War II."

"Right." Ben focused on the frame again. "And in this very frame, she kept the only picture she had of the two of them. She looked at it every day. Praying he'd come home."

Vanessa raised her pretty brow. "And?"

"He did." Ben let the rest of the story spill out all at once. "They married and had a family and lived happily ever after. The end."

"Why didn't they keep the frame?"

Ben shrugged. "They remodeled and sold it at a swap meet. Kept the picture for the kids."

Vanessa laughed. "That's it?"

"It's not always a Hollywood ending." Ben picked up another frame, one that was slightly turned so Vanessa couldn't see it. "And . . . what about this one?"

The moment Vanessa looked, she saw what Ben had done. The frame held a photo of the two of them. Something he'd done while back home in Marietta.

"Ben . . . that's us." Vanessa took the frame. She was clearly shocked. "How did you . . . ?"

"Well, let's just say for that one . . . the story has only just begun."

They headed to the register then and Ben bought four additional frames. He looked at Vanessa. "Old frames are like Christmas itself. They both hold the images we'll remember for a lifetime."

"Maybe you need your own book." She held on to his elbow as he paid.

When they left the store, carolers were singing on Old Town Square. "Seems only right," Ben teased her. "I mean, they might not invite us to sing, but . . ."

"Absolutely. We have to listen."

A small crowd had gathered by then. Ben and Vanessa found a spot near the back, several feet from the audience. A place where it felt like just the two of them.

The stars shone bright overhead, and the voices of the carolers filled the air. Again, Ben put his arm around her. The group finished one song and started "The Christmas Song." One of Ben's favorites.

He lowered his face to her level and whispered, "You cold?" He stood behind her and slipped his other arm around her, too.

"Not now." She turned in his arms so she could see him. And like that the moment was theirs alone. Ben worked his fingers into her hair. He was about to kiss her when out of nowhere, the Sidewalk Santa walked by ringing his bell again.

The sound caught them off guard and they both burst out laughing. Ben shook his head. "Busy guy."

"Definitely." She bit her lip. "I don't really want to leave this, but . . ."

"Dinner reservations?" He laughed. "You're right." He put his hand alongside her cheek. "Can I take a rain check on this moment?"

"I hope so."

They made their way inside Emilio's, Old Town's best Italian restaurant. Before they were seated, Vanessa's expression changed ever so subtly. "I have to tell you something."

"Okay." Ben couldn't imagine this being bad news. Not after the moment they'd just shared.

"Sadie and I worked at the Veterans' Hall till late last night, and when we got home, she FaceTimed Hudson." Vanessa sighed. "I'm sorry. Today she was gone with Ella and Cami before I woke up. They were headed to Fort Benning. The rest of the day was more decorating and filling baskets and—"

"And you haven't told her." Ben laughed. "I'm trying to imagine the look on her face when we show up at the dance tomorrow night. 'Hello. I'm Ben Miller. Your mom and I have been talking every day for the past six months.'"

Vanessa put her hand to her face. "It's like a comedy of errors."

"It'll all work out." Ben took her hand. "Let's enjoy tonight."

THEY WERE seated at a beautiful booth near the back, and Vanessa wished the night would last forever. The window next to the booth overlooked Old Town Square and the tree. They could even hear the faint sound of songs from the carolers. "This"—Vanessa turned to him—"might be my favorite Christmas moment ever."

"It might be mine, too." Ben looked like he could spend the rest of the evening staring at her. As if he were memorizing her features.

They ate chicken piccata, and after dinner they ordered a piece of cheesecake to share. That's when Ben took her hand and ran his thumb over the bare spot on her ring finger. "This is where you wore the Christmas ring?"

"It is." Vanessa still had her wedding ring on the other hand. She was beginning to feel self-conscious about the fact. But if things with Ben kept moving in this direction, she would remove it. They had time.

Ben lifted his eyes to hers. "You haven't told me the history of it. The Christmas ring."

"I haven't?" Vanessa couldn't believe that.

"No. Just that it was a red stone with shiny diamonds. Cubic zirconia, I'm guessing."

"Probably." She leaned back in the booth. "It's a great story. My great-grandfather found the ring on D-Day."

"Wait. Actually? On D-Day?" Ben leaned forward. "How did that happen?"

Vanessa smiled. "He shared the story with me a hundred times. It was his favorite." Vanessa could picture him. Still handsome in his seventies and eighties. She was the apple of his eye back then. "He was part of the 101st Airborne Division."

"The Screaming Eagles. Okay." He looked shocked by the fact. "He told you this?"

"Every word." She took her time. "He was a paratrooper, part of the group sent in ahead of the land assault that day. The jump went wrong from the start. He and his friends were all scattered to the wind. They landed eight miles inland from Utah Beach, and a group of them found shelter in an oversize bush."

"It's hard to believe any of them survived."

"Exactly." She could still hear her great-grandfather Bill Bailey, the depth in his voice as he told the story. "A few hours before they were rescued, he felt something deep in the dirt. He dug it out and there it was. He polished it on his army pants, and in the light of the moon he could see it better. A ruby-red stone surrounded by a ring of diamonds."

"That's incredible."

Vanessa tried to imagine the moment. "Somehow holding the ring, he had the sense he just might survive. Maybe he would make it out and find a wife and raise a family. He was so moved by the piece of jewelry that he named it."

"The Christmas ring."

"Yes." Vanessa looked at the spot where Ben still had hold of her hand. "It was in the family until I lost it that day in Breckenridge." She thought back again. "After he was rescued, maybe six months later, my great-grandfather met a French woman. They fell in love and married, and she came back to Columbus, Georgia, with him. She loved him so much."

"Like a movie." Ben was taken by the story, Vanessa could see that much.

"They started their family here, and on their second anniversary he took the ring to a jeweler and had it engraved."

"Engraved? Oh. That's . . . that's special." Ben blinked. For the first time since she started the story, he didn't look lost in the history of the ring. He released her hand and searched her eyes. "What did it say?"

"It's on the inside of the band. In cursive it says *Maison*." She smiled. "It's hard to read. It means 'home.'"

"Home." Ben sounded like he was in a trance. He coughed a few times. "That's . . . that's beautiful."

"It is. And now Isaac Baker may have found it. Not just for me, but for Sadie."

Ben looked off, like maybe he wasn't feeling well. This time Vanessa took his hand, and his thumb seemed to accidentally brush against her wedding ring. At the feel of it, he pulled his hand back and slid to the edge of the booth. "I'm sorry." He smiled at her, but something had changed. "Would you excuse me for a minute?"

"Of course." The entire moment suddenly felt awkward. *What happened?* Vanessa didn't know what to do. Had she overstepped by taking his hand? That's when things seemed to change.

Ben stood and nodded to her. Then he hurried out the front door. Vanessa looked at her wedding ring and tried to imagine what was going on in Ben's head and why he had needed to leave so suddenly. Maybe it was her . . . or maybe it was him.

Maybe telling him the story had triggered old memories for him also. And perhaps that proved something he hadn't known about himself until right now. The idea that he wasn't ready to love again.

No matter how great things had seemed ten minutes ago.

BEN'S HEART was pounding out of his chest.

How could this have happened, and how come he hadn't figured it out till now? He felt sick to his stomach, his knees weak. He pulled his phone from his coat pocket and dialed his dad. "Please pick up . . . please." The words came from a desperate place in his soul. He paced to Old Town Square and back again.

He tried his dad twice more, but his phone only rang and rang. Tomorrow morning his dad would have sold the ring and that would be that. He'd have the money and be booking a trip to Italy.

And Vanessa would never see her Christmas ring again.

His heart was still racing. What was he supposed to tell her? Certainly nothing would make sense to her any more than it made sense to him. He had to get the ring back before tomorrow morning, and that meant just one thing.

His phone back in his coat pocket, Ben returned to the restaurant. Vanessa clearly knew something was wrong. Her expression told him that much. He sat down and shook his head. "I'm so sorry. I was . . . This was the best time, but . . ." His mouth was dry, his heart pounding. "I need to go back home. Tonight."

"Ben?" Her eyes told him she didn't know what to make of this. "Is it your dad?"

"He's okay. It's not that." Ben couldn't grab a full breath. "I'll explain it to you later." He took more than enough cash from his wallet and left it on the table. "Can I take you home?"

"Of course." Her tone, the look in her eyes . . . All of it was different. Like in a moment's time the closeness between them was gone. "Let's go." She gathered her purse and slipped her coat on.

Ten minutes later Ben pulled up in front of her house. He had been planning to walk her inside at the end of this night. Ask her if they could share a cup of coffee and maybe sit near her Christmas tree and talk.

Not anymore. He had to get to his father. Had to stop the sale before it was too late. He walked her to the front door and took her hands in his. "I'm sorry. Really, Vanessa. I'll call you tomorrow."

She looked like she was about to cry. "Did I do something? Say something?"

He couldn't have felt worse if someone sucker punched him. "No, no." He had no time to lose, but he had to make her understand at least this much. "It's not you. Believe me. It's just . . . something I have to take care of back home."

"Okay." Her eyes welled up, but she managed a smile. "Will you come back tomorrow? For the dance?"

The dance. Ben's heart sank to another level. "I don't know." It was the only honest answer he had. If his father went ahead with the sale—and that was his right—Ben could hardly come back to Columbus and take her to the dance. "I promise I'll explain this. Soon."

He hugged her goodbye, but their connection felt shallow, like nothing from the past week had happened at all.

Halfway to the interstate Ben tried his father again. *Please, Lord, make him answer his phone. I need Your help. Please.* Not until he was an hour into his trip did his dad pick up.

"Ben? What is it?" His father sounded worried. "I have eleven missed calls from you."

"Yes. Dad. We need to talk." Ben kept a tight grip on the wheel of his truck, his eyes on the road.

"Aren't you supposed to be on a date?" His dad's tone relaxed. "Don't tell me you're asking for advice about women." He chuckled. "I'm far too old to help you there."

"Dad, listen." Ben tried to keep his tone even. "The ring . . . the one you're selling. It belongs to Vanessa Mayfield." He barely paused to let that sink in. "It's her ring, Dad. You can't sell it."

His father hesitated. "Son, you're wrong. The ring she's looking for, it's costume jewelry. She told you so herself."

"Someone gave her bad information. She didn't know. She still doesn't know." He forced himself to stay calm. He had to make his father understand. "Dad, it's her ring. She and I were talking about it over dinner, and she went into more detail. It's been in her family for generations."

"What in the world, son?" His dad rarely sounded upset, but he did now. "Why would you even think it could be hers? You know how many rings are floating around out there? Thousands of rings in and out of antique shops all over the country every day."

A sense of peace came over Ben. His dad still had the ring. He hadn't sold it yet.

"I figured it out tonight." Ben paused. "Her great-grandfather had the word *Maison* engraved on the inside of the band. Vanessa just told me."

"Now wait a minute." This time his father raised his voice. "You're definitely wrong about that, son. I looked at it myself. With my glasses on." He spoke softer now, but the outrage remained. "That ring is old and scratched, but it's not engraved." He paused. "I'm selling it in the morning, and that's that. God brought it to me and it's mine."

"Dad." A new burst of panic pressed through Ben's veins. How could this be happening? His father was always a reasonable man, but not here. Not now. "What about the guy who's been reaching out to Vanessa? I told you about him. Isaac Baker."

"Exactly." His father sounded vindicated. "He said he found the ring. So let him find it. The one I'm selling is an entirely different piece."

"No, Dad." Ben exhaled. "Isaac said he believed the ring was at one of three antique stores in northern Georgia. That's us. Don't you see? That's Vanessa's family ring. You can't sell it."

"Listen." The conversation was over. His dad's tone made that clear. "I'm sorry, son. You're mistaken. I've been working at the store, but I'm going home to get some sleep. I have a big meeting in the morning." He hesitated. "Drive safely."

Drive safely? "Can you at least—?"

His dad was gone. The call ended. "This can't be happening." Ben slumped in his seat and picked up his speed. "I need a miracle, God. Please . . . open my dad's eyes."

He would get back to Marietta as quickly as he could, and he would be waiting for his dad out front of the store when he got there. One way or another he would convince him.

Even if he had to buy the ring himself.

Chapter 14

VANESSA COULDN'T SLEEP, SO she pulled a box of old mementos and photographs from the cabinet beneath the television. She sat on the floor not far from her glowing tree. The brokenness of the night seemed to call for this, a time to look back.

The house was quiet, the tick of her old grandfather clock in the corner the only sound. Sadie was asleep down the hall, so it was just Vanessa and the reality of how badly the night had ended. She could figure only one reason for Ben's sudden departure. When she had reached for his hand and his fingers had touched her wedding band, everything must have hit Ben all at once.

If Vanessa was still wearing her wedding ring, then he probably assumed she wasn't ready for a relationship. And that must have triggered an equal thought in Ben. That he wasn't ready either. They had both found the loves of their lives and they had both lost them.

No matter how things had seemed leading up to the dinner, the reality probably hit Ben. He really didn't want anything more than a friendship with her. End of story.

Vanessa pulled the box near and closed her eyes. *Lord, this is harder than I thought. Hold me, please. I need You.*

A sigh rattled her soul. She opened the box and there at the top was Sadie's first little Bible. The one she had when she read to Mister Bear and to her and Alan when she was in first grade and second grade and third.

How that girl had wanted to be a teacher.

The Bible was older now, an antique in its own right. She picked it up and ran her fingers over the worn imitation leather. Vanessa blinked back tears. If Sadie wanted to be a photographer, Vanessa would be nothing but proud of her. Happy for the fact. But she would always miss that little girl's passion for all things classroom.

"Mom!" From down the hall Sadie's voice pierced the silence. She sounded frantic. "Mom! Quick! Come here!"

Vanessa ran toward her daughter and into her bedroom. Sadie was sitting on the edge of the bed, tears streaming down her face. Her phone was beside her. She was crying too hard to talk, but she stood and fell into Vanessa's arms.

Vanessa's heart skipped a beat. *Not Hudson. Please, God, not Hudson.* The scene reminded her of the one that played out in their lives four years ago. She didn't want to ask, but she had no choice. "Honey, what is it?"

"Hudson . . . He hasn't called. And I heard one of the units got attacked. I mean . . . it might not be his, but what if it is?"

"No. Honey." Vanessa held Sadie closer. "Oh, Sadie." She stroked her daughter's back, and after a moment they sat next to each other on the end of her bed. "I'm so sorry. Let's pray. Right now."

Vanessa led the prayer, begging God to be with Hudson. When the prayer ended, Sadie turned to her.

"I'm scared, Mom. I don't know what to do. I can't reach him."

In the dark of the room, with the worst possible scenario hanging over them, Vanessa put her arm around Sadie and pulled her near, the way she had when Sadie was a little girl. The way she had when Alan died. "I'm here, Sadie honey. I'm here and God is with us. He's with Hudson."

"He is. I know." Sadie leaned her head on Vanessa's shoulder. "But I'm still so scared."

For a quick moment Vanessa stood and got Sadie a tissue. Then she sat beside her again. "Sadie, we've been praying for Hudson every day. He's not alone."

"I know." Her sobs subsided a bit. "Mom, please. Can you tell me that Bible verse? The one you used to say over me when I was little?"

Her words were healing to Vanessa's broken heart. After the night she'd had and after the stops and starts she'd experienced with Sadie since she'd been home from Reinhardt, this was the only place Vanessa wanted to be. Comforting her daughter and reminding her of the truth.

Vanessa closed her eyes. "First Peter 5:7. Cast all your anxiety on Him because He cares for you. He does care for you, Sadie."

She nodded. "More. Please, Mom, tell me more."

"Philippians 4:6. Do not be anxious about anything, but in every situation, by prayer and petition . . ." Vanessa repeated every Scripture on peace and comfort she knew, and then she ran through them again and again until Sadie was almost asleep.

Vanessa eased her back into bed and pulled the covers over her. She left Sadie's room without making a sound and hurried to the kitchen. There, she called Peggy, Hudson's mother.

Peggy answered right away. "Vanessa, he's okay. He's fine, honey." Relief rang in every word.

When the call ended, Vanessa hurried back into Sadie's room. Her daughter was sound asleep, curled up with her little Mister Bear. Tears filled Vanessa's eyes and she waited a moment, holding on to the sight of her.

In time, she moved closer and sat on the edge of her bed. "Sadie." She touched her daughter's shoulder. "Sadie, honey. Can you hear me?"

Sadie shifted. "Mmm." She blinked a few times and squinted at Vanessa. "Mom?"

"I talked to Hudson's mother. It wasn't his unit. And the guys who were hit are all okay."

The good news woke Sadie a little more. She sat up, the bear clutched in her hand. Vanessa hugged them both, and then, still holding Mister Bear, Sadie settled back down on her pillow. In a few minutes she was fast asleep again.

Vanessa stood and watched her daughter, sleeping with her bear the way she had when she was little. Whatever had happened with Ben tonight, God was with them. He was with them all. Especially Hudson. *Thank You, God. Thank You.*

She took a deep breath, and once more she touched Sadie's shoulder. "There," she whispered. "You're going to be okay."

THE EARLY morning air was cool and damp, but Ben didn't mind. He sat on the bench outside Millers' Antiques and waited. Where he'd been for the past hour. Once the doors to the shop were opened, things would get busy and Ben would miss his chance.

Convincing his father would happen now or never.

Finally, he watched his dad walk around the corner. After all this time, he still parked in the back lot. Front spaces were for customers, he'd always said. Now if he could just apply the same kindness to the situation with Vanessa's ring.

His father saw him and stopped for a beat. Then he shook his head and kept walking. When he reached Ben, he stopped. "Why didn't you just go inside and see for yourself?"

"I already saw it. I held it in my hands, Dad. Remember?" Ben was determined to be kind today, but they weren't off to a good start. "You can't sell that ring. It belongs to Vanessa. I know it."

Nothing short of astonishment filled his father's face. "Do you know how many antique Christmas rings there are in the world?" He shook his head. "Too many to imagine." His dad resumed his walk toward the front door.

Ben stood and caught up to him. "Vanessa described her ring to me. It's the same one, Dad."

"Then why didn't you say something the other day?" He stopped and faced Ben, no longer baffled but angry. "When you saw it?"

"Of course I wondered." Ben raised his voice now. "I mean, it looked like the ring she had lost. Of course." Ben clenched his jaw. "But I didn't know her ring was real. And I had no idea her ring was engraved. And this one is." Ben paused. "I'll buy it myself if you want. Just give me time to get the cash."

"Ben. Enough." His dad started walking again. "You'd be

wasting your money. The ring I'm selling today is *not* engraved and it's not Vanessa's. Period." He uttered a frustrated laugh. "This ring is scratched. It's old and worn on the inside. That's it." He shot a look at Ben. "There's a difference."

His options all but gone, Ben took light hold of his father's arm. "Look at me, Dad. Please."

For a quick moment, his father stopped.

"Dad, the engraved word is *Maison*. It's French. It means 'home.' Please . . . go look, Dad."

"It's not engraved." That was all his father said in response. As if the matter had long been put to rest. "The buyer will be here in an hour. I need to get to work."

Ben thought about following his dad into the store and forcing him to see the inscription. But that wouldn't work. He wouldn't see what he had already missed. Out of options, Ben walked to the rear of the building and used his key to enter the back room. How could his dad be so obstinate? So downright rude?

And what would Vanessa think of him and his father once she knew that he'd found the ring and sold it to the highest bidder?

Ben grabbed the broken bookcase and laid it on the workbench. He grabbed the loose boards and set them aside and then took a sledgehammer to the back of the piece. Venting everything he had on the stubborn thick slabs of wood. The whole time he prayed just one prayer.

That his father would have eyes to see.

Chapter 15

LONG AGO, VANESSA HAD learned how to handle pain and where to take her deepest questions. When she was a little girl, she watched her parents bring out the Bible often. And she'd seen from their example that the best way to stay close to God was to read it on her own time as well.

As a kid she used to think reading the Bible was a to-do item, something a person was supposed to do to keep in the Lord's good graces. But that wasn't how Vanessa saw reading the Bible now. Before she and Alan married, Vanessa had come to think of the Bible as God's love letter. Personally written for her. The first chapter of John declared that "in the beginning was the Word, and the Word was with God, and the Word was God."

And so it was.

After that, when she sat down and opened the covers of this book, she no longer thought of it as a task or a textbook. Reading the verses in the Bible meant having a meeting with God. He was truly alive and active in the pages of Scripture.

That morning, the day of the military dance, with Sadie still asleep down the hall, Vanessa found her Bible and settled in on the sofa. She turned to Philippians chapter 4 and read the verses she had recited to Sadie the night before. The section held more than Vanessa had quoted, more than she remembered.

And now she wanted to spend time here.

She started at the fourth verse. *"Rejoice in the Lord always. I will say it again: Rejoice! Let your gentleness be evident to all. The Lord is near."* Vanessa closed her eyes. He was near. He absolutely was.

Once more she found her spot and kept reading. *"Do not be anxious about anything, but in every situation, by prayer and petition, with thanksgiving, present your requests to God. And the peace of God, which transcends all understanding, will guard your hearts and your minds in Christ Jesus."*

The words washed over her and filled her very being with peace. She had read somewhere that it was impossible to be thankful and anxious at the same time. And sure enough, here was that very idea written in the Bible so long ago. God's promise to those who were worried or troubled. Rejoice . . . be thankful . . . take every problem to the Lord. And the peace of God that knew no bounds would guard her heart and mind in Jesus.

It was a promise.

She drew a deep breath. Before she could read further, she heard Sadie coming down the hallway. When she stepped into view, Vanessa smiled at her. "Hi."

Sadie held up her little children's Bible. "I found this on my bed."

"Yes." Vanessa smiled. "I was looking through the box from under the TV." She nodded to the container, still in the corner. "I found it in there."

Sadie came closer and took the spot next to Vanessa. For a moment she stared at the little book. "I sure loved this."

"You did." Vanessa studied her daughter.

"Back then I couldn't wait to be a teacher." Sadie set the book down on the arm of the sofa. "But now . . . I love the idea of taking pictures. Finding beauty in everything around me. People . . . pets . . . places. All of it."

Vanessa could see Sadie's joy. "I need to get you a toy camera for Christmas." They both laughed. "Your old Bible. It was just a night to remember. That's all."

"I'm so glad Hudson's okay." Sadie pressed her shoulder into the sofa and faced Vanessa. "He texted me."

Sadie put her hand on Vanessa's Bible. "You know what I miss?"

"What do you miss?"

"Waking up and seeing you reading your Bible. Early in the morning." Sadie flipped through the pages and then looked back at Vanessa. "I love that."

"The words get me through life. They always have."

For a minute neither of them said anything. But Sadie clearly had something on her mind. She met Vanessa's eyes. "Can we talk about the other day, when I cut you off? We haven't had a lot of time, but . . . tell me what you were thinking that night. Would you, please?"

There would never be a better time than now to tell Sadie the story. Every detail. "It goes back a bit."

"Okay." Sadie looked ready to listen. She settled into the sofa cushion once more.

"It started this past summer after I dropped you off for orientation. I stopped at Millers' Antiques in Marietta."

"I remember that. You looked for your ring."

"Right. But I ended up finding something else. Someone." Vanessa gave a slight shrug. "I met the owner's son. Ben Miller. He lost his wife to an illness eight years ago, and . . . well, we had a lot in common and we started a friendship."

"Since July?" Sadie sat up straighter. She didn't sound angry, just surprised.

"Yes." Vanessa wasn't keeping anything from Sadie now. Not anymore. "We would talk and text. Once in a while we'd FaceTime. And when I came to visit you, I'd stop and have lunch with Ben on the way home. Or we'd look at other antique stores in Marietta."

Sadie couldn't have looked more surprised if Vanessa had said they were moving to Mars. "And you never told me?"

"You were busy, honey. Getting used to college, writing papers. Memorizing textbooks." Vanessa sighed. "It seemed like something I should tell you in person. And then I was never sure if he and I were just a passing fancy. Nothing more than friends. I didn't want to upset you."

Remorse seemed to come over Sadie. "Mom. You're still my best friend. I'm never too busy for you." She took Vanessa's hand. "I need you."

Her words were like oxygen to Vanessa. "Thank you."

"There's more, right?"

Vanessa was going to tell her, but Sadie looked like she knew something. "Why do you ask?"

"I saw the two of you. Shopping the other day." Sadie looked guilty for not telling her sooner. "You were holding hands."

The blow hit hard. Vanessa hung her head for a few

seconds, and then she looked at Sadie again. "You were supposed to be at the mall."

"The girls and I switched plans." Sadie sighed. "At first I couldn't believe what I was seeing. And then . . . I remembered. You tried to talk to me about him, but I shut you down."

"This is all new." Vanessa blinked back tears. "I wanted to tell you way before this. I did."

"It's okay, Mom. Let's just start from here." Sadie wasn't angry, Vanessa could see that in her daughter's eyes. She was only ready to hear the rest of the story.

They moved into the kitchen and made coffee. Then they sat down and Vanessa continued. She told Sadie how she and Ben had spent the past week looking for antiques for his store and picking up donations for the military dance. "We were together every day."

"Wow . . . so . . . you must really like each other."

"I thought that." How could she explain this part to Sadie when she didn't understand it herself? "At first we were just friends, and I was trying to find a way to tell you that." She took a sip of her coffee. "We had so much fun, and then . . . well, it felt like maybe we were falling for each other. If I couldn't tell you about us being friends, how was I supposed to tell you that?"

"I didn't make it any easier." Sadie winced. "Sorry about that."

"Now I'm sort of glad I waited." Vanessa felt the emotion in her voice. "Last night Ben and I had our first date."

"First date?" Sadie raised her brow, clearly trying to find her enthusiasm. "And . . . ?"

"I thought after that, Ben and I *would* be more than friends and I'd tell you that this morning. He was supposed to go to the dance with me tonight."

The confusion on Sadie's face left Vanessa no choice but to finish the story.

She explained how in the middle of dessert Ben suddenly had to leave. "I think I scared him. Like maybe it was all too real and too serious." Vanessa looked at her left hand. "I'm still wearing my wedding ring after all." She shook her head. "I can't think of any other reason."

Sadie looked genuinely sad for Vanessa. "Mom . . . my decision not to be a teacher doesn't mean I love Dad any less. You know that, right?"

"Of course." Vanessa looked deep into her daughter's eyes. "He would be so proud of you, honey. No matter what."

"And he's proud of you, too." She paused, taking her time. "Dad's been gone four years. After the other night, I gave this whole thing a lot of thought. The truth is, Mom, if you find someone to love, I won't be upset. When I saw you and Ben the other day, of course I was confused and shocked. But one thing was very obvious."

Vanessa brushed a tear off her cheek. Her daughter was being so gracious, so kind.

Sadie smiled. "You were so happy, Mom. And I want you to be happy." She stood and Vanessa did the same thing. They hugged for a long while, and then they both sat back down. "Maybe it isn't Ben. But Dad wouldn't have wanted you alone. And I don't want that either."

"Forgive me?" Vanessa blinked away fresh tears. "I'm so sorry for not telling you."

"It's behind us." Sadie smiled through tears of her own. "I love you, Mom."

"I love you, too."

Just then Sadie's phone buzzed. She shot out of her chair, grabbed it from the kitchen counter, and checked it. "It's Hudson." Sadie's face lit up. She read the message and shot Vanessa a surprised look. "He thinks it's snowing outside. He said to step outside and look."

"It is supposed to snow tonight." A happy suspicion came over Vanessa. She played along. "I heard about the snow this morning from Maria and Leigh."

With a full heart Vanessa stood and followed Sadie to the front door. A text like that from a soldier could only mean one thing. Vanessa stayed back a few feet and watched the next few minutes play out.

THE DAYS had been colder than Sadie could remember, but she hadn't heard anything about snow. Not until her mom confirmed the fact. She opened the door expecting to see flurries, but what she saw instead nearly dropped her to the cold front porch.

Standing there in his army Ranger uniform was Hudson. Right in front of her. "You're here!" Sadie ran to him and jumped in his arms. "I can't believe it!"

He held the back of her head so their cheeks were touching. For so long he held her, swaying with her while she breathed in the same freezing air as him. When he finally released her, he looked deep into her eyes and smiled. "It's not snowing."

Tears filled Sadie's eyes and spilled onto her sweatshirt. She couldn't stop smiling. This time she put her hands on his face, and they came together in the sweetest kiss. He was here—her soldier was home. "Are you okay?"

He never looked away from her. "I've never been better."

She giggled and turned back to her mom. "Did you know about this?"

Her mother shook her head. "I had a feeling."

Sadie nodded. Of course her mother had a feeling. This was something her dad had done when he was given a last-minute trip home. More than once he had shown up on this very porch surprising the two of them.

Her mother walked up and hugged Hudson. She was half laughing, half crying. "Hudson Rogers. Have you been home to see your mama?"

"Yes, ma'am. I stopped there first."

"Good boy." Her mother patted Hudson on the back and led the way inside. "We made cookies! Sadie used the heart shape." Her mom grinned back at Hudson and Sadie. "I'm thinking she did that for you, Hudson."

They all laughed and Sadie hadn't been happier since she'd been home. She loved this. Things with her mom finally felt normal. And Hudson was no longer looking at her through a computer screen. He was here and whole and home for Christmas.

What more could she want?

OVER COFFEE and cookies, the three of them caught up, and Vanessa told Hudson about the antique dealer who had almost certainly located her Christmas ring. They celebrated the fact, and then Hudson asked about the military dance. "Is everything all set?"

"Close." Vanessa sighed. "My friends are helping this morning, and Sadie and I were going to head over to finish the baskets."

"Why don't we take care of that?" Hudson looked at Sadie. "I'd love to help."

Vanessa smiled at the young man. He'd been wired to help others since he was a young boy when he spent half the day looking for Sadie's missing kitten. "Hudson, you just got home. I think you're good to take a chair and watch."

"Nah." He chuckled. "I'm fine."

After a few more cookies, Hudson and Sadie headed out to the Veterans' Hall. Vanessa promised to follow soon. But first there was something she had to do. When the house was quiet again, she went to the living room, sat on the floor, and pulled her memory box close once more.

She looked at her left hand, at the wedding ring she'd worn since Alan placed it on her finger twenty-two years ago. "I said till death do us part," she whispered. Tears formed in her eyes. She didn't try to stop them. "But even then, I didn't want to take off the ring you gave me." She sniffed. "I wanted to wear it forever."

Like they'd done so many times before, memories of that terrible day flashed in her mind again. She'd been putting away a bag of groceries, humming a country song by

Hillary Scott—"Thy Will"—when there was a knock on the door. Sadie was at school. Cheer practice. And Vanessa hadn't been expecting anyone.

She could still see herself. A spring in her step as she opened the door. And there they stood. Two uniformed soldiers. One of them held a piece of paper. "Mrs. Mayfield." He stepped forward. "I'm so sorry."

It was hard to remember exactly what happened after that. The soldiers came inside, and she fell into the arms of one of them. Not her Alan. Not the medic, the one who had always helped everyone else. In a secret place of Vanessa's heart, she had always assumed God would give Alan a pass when he was in battle.

Because he was the one helping the other soldiers live. So certainly God wouldn't take Alan. Never Alan.

The soldiers stayed until Sadie got home. Her daughter took a moment to grasp the news, and then . . . her wailing and sobbing began. Vanessa could still hear the way Sadie yelled for her daddy. The horror of it all had stayed with Vanessa every day since.

Time would move them on to new chapters, but it would never erase the way it had felt to lose Alan. To acknowledge that there had been no sweeping goodbye, no final hug or date or last laugh together. No chance to hold him close in his final moments and tell him no one would ever love him more. No assuring him that Jesus was with him.

He was gone. His body would be returned to them days later, and he was buried in the uniform he loved.

Vanessa lifted her eyes to the window and looked beyond it. Another Scripture came to her. Psalm 121, the first verse.

"I lift up my eyes to the mountains—where does my help come from? My help comes from the Lord, the Maker of heaven and earth."

I can't do this without You, Lord. She ignored the streams of tears forging paths on either side of her face. Even if she never talked to Ben again, it was time to move on from the past. Time to acknowledge the reality she'd been living since losing Alan. They were no longer married. Her time with him had come like a very rare gift, and it had ended too soon.

Sadie was right. Alan would want her to take this next step. She sighed and very gently slid her wedding ring from her finger. The black velvet box it came in was still in the cardboard container of heartfelt mementos. Vanessa found it in the mix and opened it.

Then she did what she never imagined doing. She set her wedding ring inside, studied it once more, and closed the lid. She set the ring at the bottom of the box and set it back in the cupboard beneath the television.

A myriad of feelings came over her as she looked at her bare left hand. The deepest sorrow and the greatest certainty. But she felt something else, too. Something she hadn't thought she'd feel. After four years of missing Alan and longing for him, she felt free.

And now, regardless of what Ben chose to do today, Vanessa Mayfield was doing the one thing she definitely wanted to do. She was going to call Ben and see if he was okay. Then she was going to the Columbus Cares Military Dance.

With Ben or without him.

Chapter 16

THE BOOKCASE WAS ALMOST completely put back together, and Ben's sweat-soaked T-shirt was proof. He hadn't taken a break since he started almost an hour ago. By now, Vanessa's ring was probably sold, the twenty-five thousand dollars tucked away in some safe place where his dad could use it for the trip to Italy. There had been no way Ben could stop the sale.

His dad wouldn't hear of it.

Ben set down the hammer and grabbed the screwdriver. The bookcase was an antique, but it was solid. Now he had the back securely in place and the shelves once more secured to the interior. He was about to tighten down the screws when he heard a beep from his phone.

With the back of his hand, he wiped his forehead. Only one person would be leaving him a message today. The one person he should've called by now. Except he didn't have anything to tell her. What they had started would officially end with the sale of her long-lost Christmas ring.

Even still, he grabbed his phone and checked it. Sure enough, he'd missed her call. Ben checked his messages and there it was. A full minute from Vanessa. He dropped to the nearest old chair and played it.

"Ben . . . I guess I thought I'd hear from you by now."

He closed his eyes. If only there was a way out of this nightmare.

Her message continued. *"Anyway, if you changed your mind, I can live with that. I've loved every minute of being your friend. I don't think you were ready for more. But please call me. I can't believe we could end things like this. Whatever you're going through, Ben . . . I'm here."*

Whatever he was going through? If she had any idea what he was going through, she'd blame him for all of it. He should've rushed into the store and grabbed the ring. Proven to his dad then and there that the ring was definitely engraved. But all this time, while he worked on the bookcase, Ben had thought for sure his dad would check for himself.

Because that was the right thing to do.

Time had gotten away from Ben, and now he was almost certain it was too late. Of course, maybe he could get the name and number of the buyer and purchase it back. Whatever it took. Especially after hearing Vanessa's message. But for now Ben felt just one thing.

Complete and utter defeat.

CUSTOMERS FILED through the front door of Millers' Antiques one after another without a break. Howard didn't mind. This was what he and Ben had always hoped for a few days before Christmas. But after the fight with Ben, today didn't hold the holiday charm Howard was used to feeling.

Howard wore no Santa hat, and Gary for sure knew

something was wrong. Between sales, his cousin stared at him. "What's the story with you?"

"Nothing." Howard leaned against the back counter.

"Oh, I get it." Gary wore his reindeer antlers. Nothing ever dimmed his Christmas spirit. "You lost at chess yesterday and now you don't want to play for a week."

"That's not it."

Gary made a sweeping gesture toward the chessboard behind the counter. "It's all set up. Your move."

"I can't." Howard rang up another sale. "Merry Christmas." He waved to the young couple. It wasn't their fault things had gone so badly since last night. Ben was acting completely out of character. If he'd thought the ring belonged to Vanessa, he should have said so when Howard showed it to him.

It was like his son was so crazy in love with this woman, he had convinced himself the ring was hers. Making the matter worse, the buyer had called to tell him she was running late. *Perfect.* More time for it to sit there under the locked counter. More time for Ben to be angry with him.

For the first time that morning, there were no customers waiting to check out. Howard looked at the locked cabinet and a thought hit him. There was one thing he could do about the disagreement. He could get the ring out and prove to Ben it wasn't engraved.

Scratches did not count as engraving.

He slipped on his glasses and pulled out the green velvet box. Moving with great care, he took the ring from the box and studied the inside of the band. Scratches and smears. Worn by time, nothing more.

"Use your magnifying glass." Gary knew nothing about the situation with Ben, but he was watching from a few feet away, arms folded. "It's in the top drawer."

Howard didn't need his cousin's help. His eyes were just fine—with his glasses, anyway. Still, if he was going to prove to Gary and Ben that this ring was not engraved, he would go the distance. He pulled the magnifying glass out and held it up to the band.

At first he could see nothing different. But then . . . amidst the scratches a faint word in cursive took shape.

The word *Maison*.

"I told you." Gary chuckled. "Now you ready to play a little chess?"

Howard dropped the magnifying glass back in the drawer and grabbed his phone. "Hold on." He walked behind the counter where he could have a private moment. The woman didn't answer, so Howard left a message. "This is Howard Miller. Please . . . call me back right away. This is urgent."

The truth hit Howard as he hung up. What had he done? The way he had talked to Ben, his stubborn pride, insisting he knew the ring wasn't engraved. Now it wouldn't just take an apology to make things right with everyone.

It would take a miracle.

He could hear a line of customers needing help, but before he could walk back out to the register, his phone rang. *Good. I can fix this right now.* But instead of the woman, it was a man.

"This is Isaac Baker. I believe I sold you something important, and I need it back."

※

THE VETERANS' Hall was bustling with volunteers making final preparations and setting out trays of desserts. Maria and Leigh were helping Vanessa and Sadie wrap the baskets with cellophane and red ribbon.

Along the wall a dozen Christmas trees were decorated and lit. Garland hung from one end of the hall to the other on all sides, and twinkling lights wrapped the poles near the dance floor. The place looked more beautiful than any year past.

Not only that—Vanessa checked her clipboard—all but twelve of the hundred families were sponsored. They would start the night asking for final assistance, and Vanessa believed the right people would show up to help. God was working ahead of them.

And even though she hadn't heard back from Ben, she knew there had to be a reason. Even if that reason was simply that he was the wrong person for her. Sometimes God worked like that, too.

A stack of tablecloths in her arms, Sadie moved with Hudson to the other side of the room. The two of them worked to get the tables covered. Vanessa smiled watching them. The way they couldn't stop laughing, and the look in Hudson's eyes when he stared at Sadie. So young and in love.

Leigh and Maria approached Vanessa. "Okay. I think we've got them all." Maria grinned. "We did it, team. Time to get ready." She hesitated. "And Ben? He hasn't called or texted?"

"Did you check your email?" Leigh looked serious. "I

mean, come on. I can't believe this guy. He sure had me fooled."

Vanessa still wasn't angry with Ben. She wasn't even disappointed. Whatever it was that caused him to run, there was a reason. She would tell herself that even if she never knew why. "I think he just wasn't ready. For six months he's been nothing but kind." She looked at her friends. "I left him a message asking what went wrong. Telling him I was here for him."

"More than gracious." Leigh shook her head. Something seemed to catch her attention.

Vanessa followed a rustle of commotion and there, entering the building, was Mrs. Benson. On her scooter, no less.

"Looks like she learned how to use it." Maria chuckled. "Sweet old woman."

A few high school kids walked beside her, carrying platters of cookies. Vanessa couldn't hear what Mrs. Benson was saying, but no question she was still giving orders. The teens seemed to hang on every word, trying to get it right.

Vanessa slipped her arms around Leigh's and Maria's shoulders, the three of them watching the scene with Mrs. Benson play out. "See. That right there." Vanessa felt her spirits lift. "That's what Columbus Cares is all about."

"Helping each other." Maria smiled.

"Being family." Leigh chuckled. "Even if your family includes that bossy Mrs. Benson."

Vanessa heard a buzz from her phone. Maybe this was Ben. He would be texting to tell her he was sorry and that he would give her the details as soon as he arrived in Columbus. She hurried for her cell and stared at it.

Leigh and Maria moved close, waiting.

"It's Isaac." Vanessa's heart jumped. "He found my ring! He found it!" The three friends jumped around like third graders picked for the same team.

"Where is it?" Maria looked as thrilled as Vanessa felt.

"He should bring it here. That's only right." Leigh nodded. "If he wants the reward, tell him he has to bring it here. For the dance."

"He lives in Colorado." Vanessa shook her head at Leigh. "Funny girl."

"Sadie!" Maria called out. "Come here!"

Sadie and Hudson looked up and hurried to the group. Maria did the explaining. "The guy from Colorado . . . He found your mom's ring!"

"What?" Sadie scurried to Vanessa's side. "What did he say?"

Vanessa read the antique dealer's text. "Just that he found my ring. So I asked him where it was." Vanessa waited and all of them hovered over the phone. Just then Isaac's next text came through. It took less than two seconds for the good news to turn bad. "Oh no."

"What?" Hudson stood on the other side of Sadie. "Read it."

Vanessa held up the phone. "It's a photo. He has the wrong ring."

Sadie pulled Vanessa into her arms. "Mom. I'm so sorry."

"That's terrible." Maria put her hand on Vanessa's back. "That's not the way this is supposed to go."

"Give me your phone." Leigh reached for Vanessa's cell. "I'll talk to the guy."

"No." Vanessa slipped her phone back into her bag. "It's not the first time something like this hasn't worked out."

Leigh crossed her arms. "Talk about the Grinch who stole Christmas."

Gradually they all got back to work. Ten minutes later they were finished, the Veterans' Hall perfect. Before they headed to their cars, Vanessa shared a look with Sadie. Hudson was already loading empty boxes into his car, so it was just the two of them. "I guess I'll just have to keep praying."

"Yes." Sadie gave Vanessa a sad smile. "About the ring? Or about Ben?"

Vanessa only returned the smile. Because of all the people in the world, Sadie knew her best. That much was still true.

Chapter 17

HOWARD SAT ALONE IN his cluttered office, a place he rarely spent much time anymore. His gaze snagged on the small Christmas tree in the corner and he smiled. When Clara was still alive, this was the space where they would have deep conversations. About the store and Ben and their plans for the future.

About the trip to Italy Clara always dreamed they would take.

Anymore, it was a place to hold boxes of goods until Gary could ship them out. Items that hadn't sold as well as they'd hoped. A way to make room for the antiques that would move faster.

But today, this was the right place.

Howard leaned back in his old leather chair. Clara had bought it for him on their twentieth anniversary. The leather was cracked and worn and it didn't quite spin like before. But today it felt like a throne, and he felt like a king. He smiled at the framed photo of his wife that still sat on the desk.

"You'd be proud of me, Clara." He allowed an emotional chuckle. "Merry Christmas, darling."

This was about to be one of the best days of Howard Miller's life.

There was a knock at the door. It was about to go down.

"Come in." Howard stood, but he didn't move from behind the desk.

A moment later, Sheila Parker entered the office. She was maybe in her fifties, the distinguished investor, here for the Christmas ring. "Howard Miller?"

"Yes. You must be Sheila." He pointed to the seat opposite him on the other side of the desk. "Please. Have a seat."

"Thank you." She sat and Howard did the same. Sheila smiled, but her expression was all business. "I have the cashier's check right here. I don't have long. If you don't mind."

Howard released a long sigh. "Sheila, I'm sorry you had to come all this way."

"It's fine." The woman looked mildly concerned. "Traffic was light."

"I tried to call you." Howard gave her a slow nod. "Many times."

Sheila straightened in her chair. "I saw that. I had my ringer off."

The words he was about to say he had practically rehearsed. "Before I explain the situation, Sheila, I want you to know something." Howard stood and picked up the framed photo of Clara. He stared at it for a moment, then showed it to Sheila. "This is my wife, Clara."

Sheila was quiet.

"Clara was the love of my life." Howard found his wife's eyes in the photo. "She's no longer with me." He set the frame back on the desk and looked at Sheila. "Clara and I had just one son. Ben. He works here."

Sheila's impatience was clearly getting the better of her. "I really just want to buy the ring."

"You see, Sheila, Ben lost his wife, too. After that, my wife and I wanted just one thing. That Ben would find love again. True love."

Howard returned to his chair behind the desk, but he didn't sit.

He turned a framed piece of wood art so Sheila could see it. "See this? It's a quote from the Bible. 'Where your treasure is, there your heart will be also.'" Howard stared at it for a moment longer. "The truth is, Sheila, there are gifts more important than money. Diamonds more precious than jewels."

Overcome, Howard threw out his arms and grinned at the woman. "Merry Christmas, Sheila. I'm sorry you drove all this way."

"I . . . I said I don't live that far. I'd just like the—"

"Sheila. The ring is not for sale." Howard chuckled. "Not today. Not ever. You see, it doesn't belong to me. It belongs to someone else."

Disappointment came over Sheila, but it didn't last long. She sighed. "I figured there was a problem. I was just hoping . . ." Her eyes lit up a little again. "What about that writing desk in the front window? Is that for sale?"

"In fact, it is." Howard ushered Sheila to the door and out of his office. "You can talk to my clerk, Gary, about that. He'll be happy to help you."

"I guess that's why I'm here today."

"I guess so."

"Howard." Sheila turned around and met his eyes. "Whoever you're giving that ring to, you must love them an awful lot."

Howard's heart was full. "More than you know."

When she was gone, he took the ring from the top drawer of his desk. It was time to get it to its rightful owner.

FINALLY, THE bookcase was finished.

Ben wasn't sure what to do next. He had planned to be in Columbus by now, and he needed a shower before he could do anything. It was two thirty, and still he hadn't heard from his father. No apology, no explanation. Nothing.

But then, how was he any better? He should've gone into the store and talked it over with his father. Asked him to take a second, closer look at the ring. Especially after raising his voice at his dad this morning.

Instead, he'd been back here all this time, only making things worse.

Whatever. He still had no idea what he was going to tell Vanessa. Ben was about to leave through the back door when his father came hurrying in from the storefront. "Ben! Ben, don't leave."

"Dad." Ben slumped a little. "I'm sorry. I shouldn't have

talked to you like that." Ben's shirt was damp with sweat and sawdust. He must've looked like a mess.

"Wait. I have something—"

"No, really. The truth is, Dad, the ring belongs to you. You bought it. Or... I guess by now it belongs to the buyer."

His father came a few steps closer. "Son, you don't owe me an apology."

"Yes, but—"

"The whole thing was my fault." His dad was closing the gap between them, moving closer still. "The ring was engraved, just like you said. And it hit me. Something your mother used to say. A quote from Scripture. 'Where your treasure is, there your heart will be also.' That's the truth."

"You saw the engraving?" Ben couldn't understand. Why hadn't his father run out here to tell him that hours ago? "Why...?"

"I needed to speak with the buyer before I could come tell you. But that's done now." His dad smiled, his eyes watery. "Love, son. Love is the greatest diamond in the rough. Especially at Christmastime."

His father pulled the green velvet box from his pocket and handed it to Ben. "Italy will have to wait."

Ben wasn't sure whether to laugh or cry. He took the box with shaking hands. "Are you serious?"

"It's not mine to sell." His dad shrugged. "Not mine to give away." A grin tugged at his lips. "Go give it back to Vanessa."

His words triggered another kind of reality. The dance was in three hours. He hugged his dad hard and took him by the shoulders. "Thank you. Thank you so much." Then he hurried for the door. "I just might have time to get there. I gotta run."

They shared one more smile and then Ben flew out the door, the ring in his pants pocket. All he could do now was pray Vanessa would understand, that she'd forgive him for the way he'd acted. His smile remained as he drove home and got ready. He had a feeling she just might. But first things first.

He had to get to the dance.

VANESSA WALKED Sadie and Hudson to the front door half an hour before the dance was set to begin. Hudson wore his dress blues and Sadie looked stunning in a floor-length pale blue dress, one she'd bought last summer for this special night. At the time she had hoped Hudson would be home for Christmas, but she had known better than to count on the idea.

Now, though, in what was the greatest gift for Vanessa's daughter, Sadie and Hudson were setting out to the dance together. Hudson hurried to his car and brought something back. A cream-colored wrist corsage.

Through teary eyes, Vanessa smiled, watching them. Ben's words ran through her mind again. *"Because every girl deserves a corsage."* Seeing Sadie and Hudson was like watching a flashback of Vanessa and Alan at the beginning. Young and in love, all of life ahead of them.

"You sure you don't want us to wait?" Sadie hugged Vanessa before they set off.

"No. You go." Vanessa's hair and makeup were ready,

but she still needed to get dressed. "I'll be right behind you."

When they were gone, Vanessa did the one thing she'd been longing to do. She sat by the Christmas tree and prayed for Ben. He still hadn't called, and with every passing hour she had no idea what to make of the situation.

No matter what had happened, she knew Ben, knew his character and kindness. One day what had happened last night would make sense. Even if this wasn't how tonight was supposed to go. He wasn't the Grinch who stole Christmas. He was a man who had made everything about the past six months more beautiful than Vanessa could have dreamed.

Vanessa pulled up his text messages and scrolled back to one he'd sent not long ago. A video message. She was smiling even before she hit play, and there he was. The man she had fallen for. She could admit that fully, now that it looked unlikely they would ever find their way back together.

The video message came to life.

Ben's image smiled at her. "Hi there! Okay, so the dance is two weeks away and ... well, I can't wait to see you. I have a feeling this is going to be the best Christmas of my life. Maybe it'll be the best Christmas of your life, too. Oh, and did I mention I'm a good dancer? Because I am. I really am." He laughed. "Anyway, let's talk later."

At the end of the video, Ben's image froze. Vanessa stared at him. "Wherever you are tonight, Ben, I hope you know how much I cared."

She sighed and got ready for the dance. As she left the

house she looked down at her hands. She had no Christmas ring, no wedding ring, and no corsage. But she was going to have a good night anyway. A hundred families were about to get the help they needed this Christmas.

And at the end of the day, that was what tonight was about.

Chapter 18

THE POLICE OFFICERS KEEPING an eye on Interstate 85 south that night must've caught a glimpse of Ben and known he needed a pass. A Christmas gift, maybe. Because he took the whole trip ten miles over the speed limit. He would've gone faster if it would've been safe.

He wore a dark suit and tie and a white dress shirt, and again he stopped at the florist when he got into town. They were just closing. The woman working behind the counter grinned at him. "You're Vanessa Mayfield's friend, right?"

Ben paid for his purchase. "I hope so!"

And with that he hurried out. He pulled into the Veterans' Hall five minutes after the evening's program was set to begin. A few stragglers were making their way from their cars to the entrance. Ben jogged past them all and ran into the hall.

The lights were dim and Christmas filled the room. He waited for his eyes to adjust. Every table was full of people in their celebratory best, but where was Vanessa?

Then he saw her. She was taking the stage, walking to the center with a microphone. She looked like a vision, and

Ben had a thought he couldn't deny. He wanted to spend the rest of his life with her.

If only she could forgive him.

"Welcome to the Fourth Annual Columbus Cares Military Dance." Vanessa wore a long deep red dress. The sight of her left Ben in something of a trance.

Between bursts of applause, she welcomed the attendees, thanked her volunteers, and moved straight to the families being sponsored. "Columbus Cares was a dream of mine, and tonight you have made that dream come true. Thank you."

Ben watched her check her clipboard. "Our goal tonight was to see a hundred families sponsored. Besides the basket of generously donated gifts and gift cards, each family will receive a hundred dollars. The cost of sponsorship. Right now, we need just five more sponsors to make sure we take care of every military family's needs."

With that, a few hands shot up. As people volunteered, Vanessa kept track. Ninety-seven, ninety-eight, ninety-nine. "We're just one short now." Vanessa looked around the room.

Ben couldn't hold back. He stepped forward into the light near the stage and looked straight at Vanessa. "One hundred." He held up his hand.

The room erupted into applause, but Vanessa clearly had to work to hide her shock. She thanked everyone and told them that the food tables were open. The dancing could begin.

Vanessa took the stairs on the side of the stage and came straight to him. The hurt in her eyes was enough to make

Ben physically sick. She kept more distance than usual. "Thank you. For your support."

"Listen." Ben thought about moving closer to her, but he changed his mind. She deserved an explanation. "Vanessa, I'm sorry. I never should've left like that."

"I called you." She still had walls up. He'd never seen her like this.

"I know. I can tell you everything." He glanced back at the door. "Come with me. Please."

He led her to a table near the door where he took the white corsage from its box and slid it onto her wrist. He didn't have to tell her how he felt about corsages. Her eyes told him she already knew. And she appreciated the gesture. But that didn't mean things were okay. Not yet.

Ben motioned for the exit. "Let's talk outside, okay?"

He had no idea how the next ten minutes were going to go, but he was encouraged by this much at least. She was wearing his corsage. And she was following him.

AS SOON as they left the building, Vanessa stopped short and looked up. It was snowing! Something that happened in Columbus only a handful of times since Vanessa was a little girl. The light dusting fell like something in a snow globe.

She laughed and held out her hands. "I can't believe this."

"Right on cue." Ben was trying. She would give him that much.

He led her around the corner to a quiet garden. A gazebo

stood nearby, but they didn't make it that far. "The other night. Vanessa, it was all my fault, but I had to leave."

She felt her hurt start to fade. Whatever he wanted to say, she would listen.

"I had to get back to Marietta before it was too late."

"Too late for what?" Vanessa shivered a little.

"To stop a certain sale." He searched her eyes. It looked like he wanted to take her in his arms, but he was still trying to make her understand what happened.

"At your store?" Vanessa blinked the snowflakes from her eyelashes. Inside the hall the music began to play.

"Yes." He was working hard to explain himself. "When I went back home, before our date, my dad showed me the piece he was about to sell. The one I told you about."

"Twenty-five thousand dollars? That one?"

"Yes. Only it wasn't just a special antique. It was a ring. And at first, I thought nothing of it. I never dreamed it might be yours."

Vanessa felt her pulse quicken.

Ben took a step closer. "But then at dinner you said it was engraved. *Maison*. And that word was on the ring my dad was going to sell the next morning. I saw it myself." He paused. "In that moment I knew it was your ring, and all I could think was that I had to get home. Had to stop the sale before it was too late."

"But . . . my ring was costume jewelry. The appraiser told my mom . . ."

"No. The appraiser was wrong." Ben shook his head. He pulled a green velvet box from his pocket and handed it to Vanessa. "Open it."

Her hands were shaking now, but not from the cold night air. Not from the snow. She took the box and opened the lid and there ... after all this time, since that day at Breckenridge ... there was her Christmas ring. The one her great-grandfather had found on D-Day ... the one that would someday belong to Sadie.

Tears filled her eyes and spilled onto her cheeks. "I ... I can't believe it. How in the world? How could it ... ?" She slipped it onto her finger and looked at Ben. "Is this a dream?"

Ben moved closer. He took her into his arms. "I'm in love with you, Vanessa Mayfield."

She couldn't get over any of this. The ring sparkled on her finger. "How did your dad ... ?"

"It's a long story." He pulled her closer still, the snow lightly falling on their cheeks.

Something hit her, the words he'd just spoken. "Wait ... What did you say?"

He framed her face with his hands. "I said ... I'm in love with you."

And in that moment, Vanessa knew she'd stay with Ben Miller all the days of her life. The past day and all her uncertainty fell away. "So ..." Her tone was playful now, the miracle of the moment more than she could take in. "Sorting through antique rings, were you? Interesting."

Ben must have known just what she was alluding to, because he grinned and played along. "That's what you do. When you're thinking about getting married."

Their eyes held and with the big band Christmas music coming from inside, Ben eased his fingers into her hair and kissed her, their lips warm against the cold of the snowy evening. The kiss took her breath, the way she had always known it would.

If they ever got to this point.

And now, here they were. "I'm not dreaming, right?" She lifted her face to the falling snow and then looked at him again.

"You tell me." And with that, he kissed her again. Longer this time.

Vanessa looked at her Christmas ring and then back at Ben. "God answered my prayers."

Ben didn't blink, didn't look away. "He answered mine, too." He slipped his arm around Vanessa's shoulders. "It's freezing. Let's get you back inside."

The moment after they entered the building, Vanessa saw Sadie look their way. Their eyes held for a long beat, and then Vanessa watched her daughter excuse herself from Hudson and the friends she was standing with.

Beside her, Ben had hold of her hand. He didn't have to ask. He could obviously tell this was Sadie heading their way.

"She knows?" he whispered.

"She does." Vanessa held back her tears this time. Introducing her daughter to a man other than Alan was not something she had ever planned to do. Still, here they were, and all she could do was believe Sadie would see in Ben what she herself had seen in him from the beginning. Not just that he looked like Chris Pratt in *Guardians of the Galaxy*. But more than that. How Ben was a godly, kind man. Someone they could both trust.

Sadie reached them. She turned to her mom first and

immediately noticed the Christmas ring. "Mom! How did you . . . ?"

"Ben found it. I'll tell you later." Vanessa hugged her daughter. "Sadie, I'd like you to meet Ben Miller."

Tears flashed in Sadie's eyes, but her smile was genuine. She held out her hand and then changed her mind and hugged Ben. "Nice to meet you, Ben."

"Nice to meet you, too." Ben clearly understood the depth of the situation. "I've been looking forward to this."

Sadie nodded. "Me, too."

Hudson walked up then and Vanessa introduced him as well. Ben shook Hudson's hand. "Thank you for your service, Hudson. We'd be nothing as a country without people like you."

A glimmer of light filled Sadie's teary eyes, and Vanessa could tell—Sadie liked Ben already. The four of them moved to the dance floor.

"Hudson's quite the dancer." Sadie's tone was light, her spirit clearly filled with joy. She grinned at Vanessa. "Not sure you knew that."

"Well." Vanessa gave Ben a flirty look. "I think the real test is going to be which of the guys can dance better. Ben here . . . he's got some moves, right?" She led Ben out onto the dance floor next to Sadie and Hudson. "That's what you told me. Remember?"

Ben chuckled, reluctant as Georgia snow in December. "I was teasing. Didn't I say that?"

"You didn't."

Both couples began to dance, and from across the way, Vanessa saw Maria and Leigh give her a thumbs-up. With her hand Leigh made the phone call sign and mouthed, *Call me later.*

Vanessa laughed and Ben followed her gaze. "I think Leigh wants answers."

"She can wait." Vanessa slipped her arms around Ben's neck and stayed close to him that way through the entire song.

Hudson and Sadie showed off their own moves and even drew an audience. But when the song ended, Vanessa still hadn't noticed whether Ben could dance or not. It didn't matter.

He was here and he was in her arms. God had brought him back to her, and God had found her Christmas ring, too. More than that, Ben was in love with her. And she was in love with him. Sadie had met Ben and she liked him.

Vanessa could never ask for a better Christmas than that.

Four Years Later—Christmas Eve

Vanessa still couldn't believe how fast time had flown. In the spring she and Ben would be married four years. The engagement had been fast, but she and Ben were good with that. Time was short. They knew that better than anyone.

After a lifetime in Marietta, Georgia, Howard Miller had taken a liking to Columbus, and with the proceeds from selling the antique shop, he and Ben had purchased twice the space in Old Town. Howard's cousin Gary had moved to Columbus, too. They were all one big family now. And Millers' Antiques was not just an antique store that specialized in vintage Christmas pieces. They also had a bookstore. One that featured Christmas books.

Across the church Vanessa saw Howard and Gary sitting in the third row. She couldn't get enough of the two. She had even learned to play chess. Mostly so Howard would have someone to beat.

The music began to play, and one by one the couples in the bridal party came down the aisle. Ella and Cami and Bella, from Reinhardt. Every one of them was beaming.

After all, they had more than a wedding to celebrate today. Hudson Rogers was home for good. He had finished his four years with the Rangers, and now he was part of the training team at Fort Benning.

For a moment Vanessa looked down at her hands, at the Christmas ring on her right finger and the vintage diamond wedding band on the other. Sadie hadn't wanted the Christmas ring yet. Maybe when she gave birth to her first child a few years from now, she had told Vanessa. That was fine. Vanessa had gone without it for years. She was more than happy to wear it now.

She looked around again. Yes, God had answered all her prayers. Life hadn't turned out how either she or Ben had planned. But God's plans were still good. Better than Vanessa or Ben ever could've dreamed.

Every now and then, she and Ben would take a walk and try to imagine what their lives would've been like if she hadn't come through the doors of his store for that Christmas-in-July sale. What if Sadie hadn't gone to Reinhardt or Vanessa hadn't needed gasoline right at that Marietta stop?

But there was no point thinking about such things. God had ordered their steps and here they were. At another momentous occasion, one Vanessa had prayed about since Sadie was born.

A different song began to play, the traditional wedding march. The doors at the back of the church opened and there she was, her Sadie girl. She was dressed in the most gorgeous white gown, and holding her hand in the crook of his arm was the man Vanessa loved.

Ben Miller.

Vanessa stood with the other guests, and her eyes met Sadie's. They had survived the unthinkable, and now they would celebrate the greatest gift of all. The gift of love. Vanessa turned to look at Hudson. He couldn't hold back his tears as he watched Sadie walk down the aisle to him.

When Sadie and Ben reached the front of the church, Sadie hugged him and kissed his cheek. "Thank you," she whispered.

And with that, Ben took his spot beside Vanessa. The two held hands and Vanessa savored the feeling of him beside her. Ben was not only her best friend, but the one she would grow old with. Her husband. The man who loved her daughter like his own.

In fact, over the past four years, Ben and Sadie had grown very close. She was his favorite tennis partner, and he was her confidant when she needed a father's advice. No, Ben would never replace Alan. But Sadie had come to love him very much.

They had all agreed that if God could find Vanessa's missing Christmas ring, if He could bring Vanessa and Ben together and build a bond between Sadie and Ben, then truly He could do anything. Even this wedding here today.

They were all home now. Where they belonged. Because home wasn't a place—it was the people Vanessa loved. Yes, the word her great-grandfather had chosen was the right one, for sure.

Home.

It was all part of the miracle. The one Vanessa and Sadie had prayed for on a snowy hill in Breckenridge. A miracle that Vanessa would thank God for every day.

For as long as she lived.

A Note to Readers

DEAR READER FRIEND,

I hope this finds you grabbing a tissue and smiling at the beauty of love at Christmastime. I sure enjoyed the emotional journey of traveling with Vanessa Mayfield and Ben Miller through the pages of this story. I could see them, feel their broken hearts, and agree with them on their love for the military. These characters will live on in me, so I have to love them . . . and I do. I never wanted *The Christmas Ring* to end. I hope you feel the same way!

You may know that *The Christmas Ring* is also a Christmas movie this holiday season! We will be in theaters everywhere on Thursday, November 6, so we can have a Christmas party together—you and me! Come fifteen minutes early and there will be Christmas caroling and Christmas trivia to share with other Karen Kingsbury fans at whatever showing you attend. Take your friends and truly make it the first Christmas party of the season! Wear your favorite Christmas sweater and let's celebrate by making this movie a big box office hit!

As for Christmas itself, maybe this year you can take an antique item down from the shelf and share it with the younger generation. Or here's an idea . . . get that special person an antique from your local antique store . . . and a copy of *The Christmas Ring*.

What a perfect, one-of-a-kind way to give a special gift this year! If you'd like the book autographed or personalized, visit my online bookstore at KarenKingsburyBookstore.com. All my books are available there, in addition to wherever books are sold.

In closing, thank you for reading *The Christmas Ring*. I pray it stays with you and that you feel the Lord's loving arms around you as you read it again and again. He gave me this story so that I could give it to you. To Him be the glory!

Finally, if you are seeking a faith like Ben's and Vanessa's, find a Bible-believing church and get connected. There is a reason you came across this book. God is always at work connecting, speaking, helping us see Him and hear Him. Maybe reading this book was that moment for you.

Merry Christmas and may the Prince of Peace give you and yours a forever faith, hope, and love this Christmastime and always. To keep the conversation going, visit me online @KarenKingsbury on Facebook, Instagram, X, YouTube, and TikTok!

Much love until next time,

Karen Kingsbury
www.KarenKingsbury.com

Acknowledgments

The Christmas Ring was an idea that came together quickly! It never would've happened without the help of so many people along the way. I simply cannot leave it without giving thanks where it is so deeply deserved.

First, a special thanks to my amazing Thomas Nelson publishing team, including the keenly talented Amanda Bostic, along with so many others! When I told Amanda I had a book for this Christmas, she caught the vision and ran with it! Thank you, Amanda, for trusting me about making my deadline and getting this turned around so quickly.

Also, thanks to Rose Garden Creative, my design team—Kyle and Kelsey Kupecky—whose unmatched talent in the industry is recognized from Los Angeles to New York. Very simply you are the best in the business! My website, social media, video trailers, movie trailers, newsletters—along with so many other aspects of my life—are top of the business because of you two. Thank you for working your own dreams around mine. I love you and I thank God for you every single day.

A huge thanks to my sisters, Tricia and Susan, along

with my mom, Anne. You give your whole hearts to helping me love my readers. Tricia, as my executive assistant for nearly twenty years, and Susan, as the president of my Facebook Official Online Book Club and event coordinator. And Mom, thank you for being Queen of the Readers. Anyone who has ever sent me an email and received a response from "Karen's mom" is blessed indeed. The three of you are making a tremendous impact in changing this world for the better. I love you and I thank God for you always!

Thanks also to my son, Austin, for helping me navigate the world of D-Day. You helped me understand World War II leading up to that day and the impact that followed—all of which I needed if *The Christmas Ring* was going to be rooted in a very beautiful past. Thanks for making it as fascinating and heartbreaking as it is. Working with you was a blast!

Thanks to EJ for praying for me every day while I was writing this book, and to Tyler for doing more than his share of the moviemaking, producing, and directing for *The Christmas Ring* movie.

Also, thank you to my office assistant, Aurora Galvin. You create space for me to write! My storytelling wouldn't be possible without you.

I'm also grateful to my Team KK members, who step in at the final stage in writing a book. The galley pages come to me, and I send them to you, my most dedicated reader friends and family. You are my volunteer test team! It always amazes me the typos you catch at the final hour. Thank you for loving my work, and thanks for your availability to read my novels first and fast.

Also, my books only happen with the help of my family, especially my amazing husband, Donald. Honey, thank you for your spiritual wisdom and leadership in our home, and thanks for talking through books like this one from outline to editing. The countless ways you help me when I'm on deadline make all the difference. I love you!

And a special thanks to a man who has believed in my career for two decades, my amazing former agent, Rick Christian. From the beginning, Rick, you told me to dream big, set my sights high. Movies, TV series, worldwide reach. All of it for God and through Him. You imagined this, believed it, and prayed for it alongside my family and me. You saw it happening and you still do! You have officially retired and turned the reins over to my new and current agent, Bryan Norman. Thank you for your help in that.

Bryan, thank you so much for stepping in with no warning, as this story came to me practically overnight. Thank you for your kind heart and exceptional understanding of finding the right publisher for *The Christmas Ring*. You are brilliant, just as Rick said you would be. This is only the beginning!

Finally, my greatest thanks to God Almighty, who is First and Last and all things in between. I write for You, through You, and because of You. Thank You with my whole being.

Discussion Questions

1. We first see the Christmas ring in the hands of Bill Bailey, the young member of the Screaming Eagles 101st Airborne Division, as he is paratrooping into France on D-Day. What connection do you have with D-Day or World War II?

2. Is there an object of great meaning that has been passed down the line in your family? Tell about it. Why is it meaningful?

3. We first meet Vanessa Mayfield on a winter trip to Breckenridge, Colorado. She and her daughter, Sadie, are on an adventure of healing after losing their husband and father. How have you handled a loss in your life? Why is that loss especially hard during the holidays? Talk about that.

4. When a loved one is no longer here, how do you keep that person present in your Christmas celebrations? What Bible verse has brought you comfort in this?

5. The next time we see Vanessa, Sadie is headed to college a few hours away, all grown up. Have you experienced the love of a child and ultimately the letting go of that child? How did God get you through that time?

6. How do you best identify with Vanessa Mayfield? In what ways are you like her?

7. Perhaps you are the college student (or were at one time) who is moving out to find life beyond your family home. How do you keep connected with family throughout the year and at Christmastime?

8. The Bible says in the Ten Commandments, "Honor your father and mother." How is that illustrated in this book? And how do you attempt to live this out?

9. Ben Miller has a joyful heart and a love for his father, poetry, and antiques. What do you like most about Ben Miller and why?

10. Sadie is a freshman in college once the story kicks into gear. What advice would you give Sadie if you could? How would you encourage her?

11. Ben likes to make up stories about antiques. Think of an old item in your home. What story would you make up about it?

12. Most of us have an old object we've kept from gen-

erations past. Maybe a Bible or an old wall hanging. Perhaps a teacup. What is something you've kept from your parents or grandparents? Share the significance of that item.

13. Along the way, Vanessa tries to tell Sadie about Ben, but the timing is never right. Have you—or has someone you know—found a second chance at love? How did the pieces come together for the family?

14. Vanessa is drawn to Ben's kindness and humor. When they are pulled to the front of a coffee shop to sing an impromptu Christmas carol, Ben is all in. How do you find fun and spontaneity at Christmastime?

15. Sadie loves the tradition of watching a Christmas movie with her mom. What is one of your favorite Christmas movies and why?

16. Another tradition mother and daughter share is the making of Christmas cookies. Share three traditions you keep at Christmas or during the holiday season. How long have they been in the family, and why are they important to you?

17. When Ben learns that the ring his father is about to sell is actually Vanessa's missing Christmas ring, he immediately leaves town to stop the sale. How would you have handled that moment? And when did you have to take drastic measures to make a situation right?

18. When Ben abruptly leaves town before his and Vanessa's date is officially over, she forgives him. She does this because she cares about him. Forgiveness is the fabric that brings about a beautiful Christmas for us all. Is there someone in your life whom you could forgive this Christmas? How might you do that?

19. Once Howard understands that the ring is indeed Vanessa's special heirloom, he stops the sale. He explains that "where your treasure is, there your heart will be also." These are the words of Jesus from Matthew 6:21. What does this Bible verse mean to you?

20. One of the most poignant scenes in the book is when Sadie meets Ben for the first time. They both handle the moment with grace. Tell about someone who joined your family and how that person was loved by you and others. Why is love so important always, but especially at Christmastime?

21. How did you like the ending of *The Christmas Ring*? Would you like to be part of the crowd celebrating at the dance that night? Does this remind you of your story? Explain.

22. What does Christmas mean to you?

About the Author

#1 *New York Times* bestselling author Karen Kingsbury is America's favorite inspirational storyteller and filmmaker, with more than twenty-five million copies of her award-winning books in print. Her last dozen titles have topped bestseller lists, and many of her novels have been developed into major motion pictures.

With the recent formation of Karen Kingsbury Productions, Karen and her team released their first theatrical feature, *Someone Like You*, in 2024. The movie received the coveted "Certified Hot" from Rotten Tomatoes for its wildly popular audience rating. Her Baxter Family series was developed into a TV series, *The Baxters*, now playing on Amazon Prime Video. Karen and her team are currently working on a theatrical Christmas movie for 2025, and their third theatrical film is slated for 2026. She and her husband, Donald, live in Tennessee near their children and grandchildren.

✳

Visit her online at karenkingsbury.com

- @karenkingsbury
- @karenkingsbury
- @karenkingsbury
- @karenkingsbury1
- @karen_kingsbury

BASED ON THE BESTSELLING NOVEL
KAREN KINGSBURY'S
THE CHRISTMAS RING
STARRING JANA KRAMER
& BENJAMIN HOLLINGSWORTH
SEE THE MOVIE NOW!
SCAN FOR
SHOWTIMES
& AVAILABILITY

THE HIT MOVIE NOW AVAILABLE ON DIGITAL, BLU-RAY & DVD

FROM #1 NEW YORK TIMES BESTSELLING AUTHOR
KAREN KINGSBURY

someone like you

LOVE IS BEAUTIFUL...EVEN IN THE BROKEN PLACES

Buy now at someonelikeyou.movie

YOU WERE SEEN

Join the movement and see how love can change a life.

Spread gratitude and generosity with a You Were Seen card.

Jesus said they will know
we are Christians by our love.
You can do that one person at a time.
One generous tip at a time.
One You Were Seen card at a time.
Visit youwereseen.com

Karen Kingsbury's
One Chance Foundation

The Kingsbury family wants to thank you for donating to the One Chance Foundation! Here, 100% of your tax deductible donation goes to bring children home to their forever families. Just think about it. For the price of a weekly latte, you can change a child's life forever.

Visit
karenkingsbury.com/foundation

AS SEEN ON
People
abc NEWS